"I wanted to come home with answers,"

Matt said, sensing Sarah's tension, as if she wanted this just as much as he did. They both glared at the closed door. "I don't like dead ends."

Neither did Sarah, especially when it meant so much to him. "You did a good thing today, Matt." Her voice was warmly encouraging. "Don't beat yourself up because you couldn't solve a forty-year-old problem in one day."

He had to smile, because that was exactly what he was trying to do. He took her arm to pilot her back down the narrow stairs, enjoying the feel of her softness against him.

"How did you get to know me so well, Sarah?"

"Just a lucky guess."

What's going on with us, Sarah? Matt wondered. This isn't supposed to happen.

But it was.

D0401155

Books by Marta Perry

Love Inspired

A Father's Promise #41
Since You've Been Gone #75
*Desperately Seeking Daddy #91
*The Doctor Next Door #104
*Father Most Blessed #128
A Father's Place #153
Hunter's Bride #172
A Mother's Wish #185

*Hometown Heroes

MARTA PERRY

wanted to be a writer from the moment she encountered Nancy Drew, at about age eight. She didn't see publication of her stories until many years later, when she began writing children's fiction for Sunday school papers while she was a church educational director. Although now retired from that position in order to write full-time, she continues playing an active part in her church and loves teaching a class of junior high Sunday school students.

Marta lives in rural Pennsylvania but winters on Hilton Head Island, South Carolina. She and her husband have three grown children and three grandchildren. She loves hearing from readers and enjoys responding to their letters. She can be reached c/o Steeple Hill Books, 300 East 42nd Street, New York, NY 10017, or visit her on the Web at www.martaperry.com.

A Mother's Wish

Marta Perry

Love Inspired®

Published by Steeple Hill Books™

STEEPLE HILL BOOKS

Steeple
Hill™

ISBN 0-373-87192-9

A MOTHER'S WISH

Copyright © 2002 by Martha Johnson

Visit us at www.steeplehill.com

Printed in U.S.A.

And we know that in all things,
God works for the good of those who love Him,
who have been called according to His purpose.
—*Romans* 8:28

This book is dedicated to my daughter Susan and her husband, David, with love and thanks.

And, as always, to Brian.

Chapter One

If he had to go into exile for the next six months, he couldn't pick a better place than this. Matt Caldwell paused outside the office of the *Caldwell Cove Gazette* and took a deep breath, inhaling a mixture of sea, salt and the rich musky aroma of the marshes. Home—Caldwell Island, South Carolina. He'd know that distinctive smell in an instant no matter where he was on the globe. Quiet, peaceful…

Pop, pop, pop. A sharp sound broke the drowsy June silence. Matt's stomach lurched. He ducked in the response that had become second nature in the last few years, adrenaline pumping, fists clenching. He had to get everyone to cover.

Fragmented images shot through his mind. He smelled the acrid smoke of explosions, felt the bone-jarring crash, heard the cries of children.

It took seconds to remind himself he was in Caldwell Cove, not on a bomb-ridden Indonesian street, seconds more to identify the sound. Some kid must be playing with caps in the lane beside the newspaper office.

A few quick strides took him around the corner of the weathered gray building. Sure enough, that's what it was. The gut-wrenching fear subsided, to be replaced by anger. Those boys were way too young to be playing with caps.

"What are you doing?"

His sharp question brought two young faces looking up at him. Their faces wore identically startled expressions. Almost identical, he realized. They had to be brothers, both towheads with round faces and big blue eyes. The older one couldn't be more than six or seven. Definitely too young to be smashing a strip of caps with a stone. He was surprised kids could even get their hands on those things now.

"We weren't doing anything." The speaker clasped his hands behind his back. His little brother nodded in agreement, blue eyes round with surprise. "Honest."

Matt frowned at the word. "Honest" was the last thing the kid was being. "You were playing with caps. Don't you know that's dangerous?"

The older boy tried a smile. "We were careful. We didn't get hurt."

"Yet." It wasn't any of his business, but these two

might injure themselves. He couldn't just walk away. "Where's your mother?"

When they didn't answer, he planted his hands on his hips and glared, waiting. "Well?"

"I'm their mother."

The woman flew around the corner as she spoke. She grabbed the boys and pulled them against her. Matt looked into eyes the same shade of blue as the kids', sparkling with indignation. Her softly rounded face and curling brown hair reminded him of a Renaissance portrait, but her expression spoke more of a mother tiger, ready to protect her young.

"Why were you shouting at my sons?" She threw the words at him.

"I wasn't shouting."

"I heard you." Her indignation sparked his own.

"Maybe you'd shout, too, if you were paying attention to your own kids." As he said it he knew he was going too far, but the emotions of the past months still rode him, erasing normal politeness. "Or don't you care what they're up to?"

The woman's mouth tightened, and she looked as if she reviewed several things she might say before responding. "I can't imagine what concern my child-rearing is to you."

"It isn't. But I have to care when I see kids in danger." He forced away the images that still haunted his dreams—of crying children huddled into makeshift bomb shelters or lying still on crowded hospital beds. "Your little angels were playing with caps."

"Caps?" That stopped her dead. She looked into her kids' faces with a hand on each one's shoulder. "Ethan? Jeffrey? Is that right?"

He waited for the quick denial again, but it didn't come. Apparently they had more trouble fibbing to her than to a stranger. The younger one looked down; the older flushed and nodded.

"We didn't get hurt, Mommy."

"Ethan, that's not the point. You know better, both of you. Where did you get caps?"

The kid looked as if he searched for an appropriate answer and didn't find it. Finally he shrugged. "We found them. In that old shed back there." He pointed toward the rear of the building, where a tumbledown shed leaned against the next building.

"I told you…" The woman stopped, and Matt saw the pink in her cheeks deepen. She probably didn't want to be having this discussion in front of him. "Go to your room, both of you. Right now. We'll talk about this in a bit."

The boys scampered around the building, and the woman looked as if she'd like to do the same. But she turned to face him, her color still high.

"I'm sorry." The words were stiff, making it clear she hadn't forgiven his sharp words. "I appreciate your concern."

He shrugged. "It's nothing." He wanted to walk

away and get on with his own affairs, but the awkward moment seemed to demand something more. He was back in Caldwell Cove now, where everyone knew everyone else, usually for a generation or two.

"I'm Matt Caldwell, by the way."

"Matt…" Her eyes widened with what might have been surprise but looked like shock. "I should have recognized you."

He started to make the polite response he always did when someone gushed that they'd seen him on television, reporting from one trouble spot or another. But she didn't give him the chance.

"I'm Sarah Reed."

Sarah Reed. Now he was the one left speechless with surprise. The woman he'd basically accused of being a careless mother was his new partner at the *Caldwell Cove Gazette.*

Sarah took a deep breath, then another, searching for some measure of calm. She'd known Matthew Caldwell was coming home to the island where his large extended family still lived. She'd known, too, that he'd undoubtedly want to discuss the investment he'd made in the *Gazette* over a year earlier, before her husband's death.

She hadn't expected to be taken by surprise like this, however. When she'd imagined their first meeting, she'd been in the office, neatly dressed in the blue suit she almost never wore, coolly prepared to discuss the fact that, since her husband's death, she was now his partner.

She certainly hadn't expected to get into a wrangle with the man before she even knew who he was. Her cheeks grew warm, and she smoothed her hands down the denim skirt that was far too casual for a first meeting with a business partner.

To do him justice, Matthew Caldwell looked just as appalled as she felt. And he managed to recover first.

"Mrs. Reed." He held out his hand, something a little rueful showing in the hint of a smile that touched his firm mouth. "I'm sure this isn't how either of us wanted to begin."

If he was prepared to be gracious, it was the least she could do, as well. She met his grip, and his hand enveloped hers, firm and strong. A faint shiver of awareness went through her at his touch, and she brushed it away.

"Perhaps we should start over," she said. "Welcome back to Caldwell Cove, Mr. Caldwell."

He grimaced. "In view of our partnership, maybe we'd better dispense with the formality. Sarah." He said her name cautiously.

She'd have preferred to hang on to some measure of distance between them, but she could hardly say so. "Fine." She took a step back, gesturing toward the building. "Why don't we continue our conversation in the office?" Maybe there she'd be able to regain her composure and get this encounter back to the way she'd imagined it. But she suspected that was a lost cause already.

She stole a glance at Matt as he walked beside her to the front of the building. She should have recognized him the instant she saw him. Maybe she had, at some level, though she hadn't identified that jolt of familiarity when she'd looked into his eyes.

She'd known of Matt Caldwell first as her friend Miranda's cousin, which was reason enough to watch for his face on the evening news broadcasts from around the globe. Then her husband had accepted Matt's investment in the paper, and she'd had more reason to be interested.

But this Matt Caldwell looked different from the tall, composed figure she'd seen standing with a microphone in front of a bombed-out building or a refugee camp. It was the same strong face, the planes of it looking as if they had been chiseled from stone, the same dark hair brushed ruthlessly back from a broad forehead.

He had the look of the Caldwells she knew already, but he had none of their casual, relaxed manner. He was dressed with a touch more formality than most men on the island, wearing chinos, not jeans, and a white shirt open to reveal a strong, tanned neck.

The lines in his face were deeper than she'd noticed on her TV screen, and the fan of wrinkles at the corners of his chocolate-brown eyes spoke of tension.

Even his hand, braced against the door as he opened it for her, looked taut, as if he might fly into action at any moment.

And he wasn't half a world away. He was here, in Caldwell Cove, disrupting her peace and interfering with her children.

The bell she'd put on the door jingled, and his hand jerked involuntarily. She frowned. What was going on with the man? He'd overreacted with her boys, no matter how wrong they'd been, and now the slightest sound seemed to affect him. Then she remembered all those danger spots she'd seen him report from and realized she knew the answer.

"Hi, Mommy." Andi looked up from the computer, and her little face grew solemn at the sight of a stranger. At eight, Andi took being the oldest very seriously, especially since her daddy's death.

Amy, at eighteen months, felt no such restraint. She banged a plastic hammer on the rail of her play yard. "Up, Mama! Up!"

"In a minute, sweetheart." She glanced at Matt and intercepted a frown. He'd probably never envisioned the newspaper office populated by a round-faced toddler clutching the rail of a play yard, nor a pigtailed little girl peering at him from behind the computer monitor.

Well, he'd just have to accept it. She couldn't afford to hire a baby-sitter every minute of the day, so the children had to be where she could watch them.

A tinge of guilt touched her. She hadn't been watching the boys closely enough. If she had, that quarrel with Matt would never have taken place. She should have realized that tumbledown shed behind the building would attract them sooner or later.

"Well." She forced a smile. "Here's the office. Is it the way you remember it?" Miranda had told her Matt had worked at the paper as a teenager, and she'd assumed that was why he'd decided to invest in it. A sentimental whim, probably—a connection to his home when he was halfway around the world.

He turned slowly, assessing the sunlit room, its worn wooden counter and elderly wall clock contrasting with the modern computers. "The computers are new. Harvey Gaylord wouldn't even have an electric typewriter in the place. He insisted on using his old upright."

"We put the computers in when we bought the paper from him." Behind the casual conversation her mind worked busily. What did he want?

It was natural enough for him to check on his investment, she assured herself. And if he had a complaint about the return he was getting on that investment—well, surely he'd realize that no one got rich running a small-town weekly. They were lucky to be able to pay the bills some months.

She ought to bring the subject up herself, instead of worrying about it, but she couldn't quite do that.

"Did you...I guess you wanted to see the operation

for yourself." It was as close as she could come to asking him outright why he was there.

"What?" He glanced up from his study of her computer, dark eyes frowning.

Wariness shivered along her nerves. There was something, some emotion she didn't understand, suppressed under his iron control.

Please, Lord. The prayer was almost involuntary. *Don't let him tell me he wants to pull out his investment. We couldn't survive that.*

"Your arrangements with my husband," she said, trying for a casualness she didn't feel. "I know they were made long-distance, through your attorney. You probably want to see the operation for yourself, while you're here on the island." She tried to manage a smile, knowing that the charm that had come so easily to Peter was totally missing from her makeup.

"Not exactly." He transferred the frown to her, and she sensed that he was searching for words to tell her something.

"Then what, exactly?" She was probably being too blunt, but she couldn't seem to help it. The newspaper was too important to her family to beat around the bush. "If you have bad news for me, I'd rather you just came out with it."

His face tightened, if that were possible, and he braced one hand against the counter. "I don't know whether you'll consider it bad news or not. The fact is, I'm here because I intend to help run the paper."

She could only stare at him. "Run the paper." She repeated the words, hearing the disbelief in her voice.

Apparently he heard it, too, because the lines in his forehead deepened as he gave a curt nod. "That's right. Run the paper. I own half of this operation, and I want to help run it."

"But…" Her mind spun. She could almost hear Peter's voice in her mind, that day last spring when he'd told her he'd accepted an investment offer from Matt Caldwell. This would be an easy solution to all their money problems, he'd said. Caldwell would be half a world away, not here, bothering them, and the money would bail them out of a tight crunch.

Now Peter's solution didn't look so easy. Their silent partner didn't intend to be silent any longer.

Matt moved impatiently, drawing her gaze back to his determined face. "Is that a problem for you?"

She took a breath, trying to ignore how off balance the man made her feel. More to the point, trying to find a tactful way of telling him she neither wanted nor needed his help. "Not a problem, exactly." Her too-expressive face was probably telling him exactly the opposite. "But it wasn't part of my understanding of what our agreement involved."

"Our agreement gives me a half share in the paper. That means I have an equal say in how it's run." He said it uncompromisingly.

Well, why wouldn't he sound sure of himself?

He'd known what he intended, after all. She was the one left unprepared by this sudden attack on her peaceful life.

She tried to summon up defenses. "But why? You have a successful broadcasting career. Why would you want to give that up to run the *Caldwell Cove Gazette?*"

His face looked closed, his brown eyes shuttered, denying her any glimpse of his feelings. "Let's say I'm ready for a break, and running the *Gazette* will give me that."

There was more to his decision than that; she could sense it. But he certainly wasn't going to confide in her. She sought desperately for another argument, any argument that might stave off this unwelcome development.

"I'm afraid you'll be bored to tears within the next month."

His smile had nothing of humor about it. "Let me worry about that."

"There's not really enough work for two. We have a couple of part-timers who help out when we need them, but otherwise, I can handle it myself." She could only hope she didn't sound desperate.

"You worked with your husband. How is it any different to work with me?"

There were so many answers to that question that she couldn't decide which one to pick. A chill touched her. She'd seen Matt Caldwell's type before—arrogant, determined, sure he was right and the rest of the world wrong. What might he do if he were running the paper? But he'd decided on this course, and he wouldn't be easily dissuaded.

"Mommy?"

She blinked, turning to Andi. She'd forgotten her daughter was there, watching them with the level, serious stare that was too old for her eight years.

"Mommy, what's wrong? What does he want?" Andi trained that solemn look on Matt.

"Nothing's wrong, honey." Nothing, except that the precarious balance she'd attained since Peter's death was seriously disrupted. Nothing, except that Matt Caldwell proposed to interfere in the running of the paper that was the livelihood for her little brood.

She looked from Andi to Amy, chewing on the rail of the play yard, thought of the two boys in their bedroom, hopefully reflecting on their misdeeds. She was all they had. She had to provide for them. If Matt presented a threat to her ability to do that, she had to find a way to defeat him.

She forced herself to meet his gaze. "This isn't a good time to discuss our business." She gestured toward the children. "Could we get together later?"

He looked ready to argue, but then he glanced at Andi and gave a reluctant nod. "When?"

No, he wasn't a man who would give up easily. "We live in the apartment behind the office. Can you come by about seven? That will give me time to get the children settled.''

"Seven it is.'' He made the words sound like an ultimatum. Then he turned and walked quickly out of the office without saying goodbye, the bell jingling as he closed the door.

Sarah let out a breath she hadn't realized she'd been holding. That didn't do any good. She couldn't relax, not yet. Matt's energy and determination still seemed to bounce from the office walls, rattling her as much as his presence had.

"Mama! Mama, up!"

She had to push herself to walk to the play yard, lift Amy, cradle her close. The baby wrapped chubby arms fervently around her neck, and then planted a wet kiss on her cheek.

Andi followed her. "What did that man want, Mommy?"

Persistence was one of Andi's strongest qualities. A good quality, but right now she could do with a little less of it. She needed time—time to think through that encounter with Matthew Caldwell, time to analyze what it would mean to them if he did what he intended.

"Nothing, sweetheart. Everything's okay."

Sarah drew in a breath. Everything's okay. She'd like to hear someone say that to her sometimes, when she struggled with the responsibility of raising four children and running a business. No one did. If Peter were here...

But dealing with trouble had never been Peter's strong suit. Peter had been laughter, charm, quicksilver. If he were here, he'd dismiss her worries with a laugh.

She closed her eyes briefly.

Father, you've helped me through everything else. Please help me handle this.

She held her daughter closer, drawing comfort from the warm, wiggling bundle of energy. She couldn't react with Peter's laughing charm, even if she wanted to. She had four children who depended on her for everything. Running the paper by herself might not be easy, but she'd proved she could make a living at it. She wasn't ready to risk that on Matt Caldwell's whim.

Her pulse gave an erratic jump as she pictured Matt, leaning toward her with tension in every inch of his body. He was tall, like the Caldwell men she knew on the island, but there the similarity ended. He was dark where they were fair, closed where they were open, driven and intense where they were casual and welcoming. How did he fit into the sprawling Caldwell clan?

She remembered something Miranda Caldwell had said once, the words dropping into her mind. *Matt's a crusader, out to set the world right. Always has been, always will be. He never gives up.*

He never gives up. The words repeated themselves uncomfortably in her mind. If she were going to best a man like Matthew Caldwell, she'd need some ammunition. And she only had until seven o'clock to find it.

Chapter Two

She couldn't win this battle. Three hours later Sarah sat at the kitchen table, staring at the contract Peter had signed with Matt Caldwell. There was no way out. Matt owned fifty percent of the paper, and he had just as much right to run it as she did.

Peter, why did I let you talk me into this?

She leaned her head in her hands, trying to think of something, anything. She hadn't wanted to take Matt's money to begin with, but Peter had been so optimistic, so sure this would solve their problems.

It was futile to hope Matt Caldwell would disappear back to Egypt, or Indonesia, or wherever his recent travels had taken him. He was here. It didn't take much insight to see that a man like him—driven, intense, competitive—wouldn't just give up and go away. She had to find a way of dealing with him.

The doorbell rang. She glanced at the clock, and her heart seemed to stop. She had to find a way of dealing with him *now*.

Sarah stole a quick glance through the small window at the top of the door just to be sure, then took a deep breath. It was Matt Caldwell, all right. He carried a manila folder and wore an expression of suppressed impatience. He looked ready to take over as editor in the next ten minutes.

She rubbed her palms down her skirt, then grasped the knob. She could handle this.

Please. She sent up a fervent, wordless prayer and opened the door.

Matt gestured with the folder by way of greeting. "I have my copy of the contract."

"Please, come in."

His quick stride brought him into her living room, and Sarah had to fight an instinctive desire to push him right back out again. He was too big, too over-powering—he filled up the room with his masculine presence, and everything about him seemed alien and disturbing.

Well, alien or not, she'd have to find a way to deal with him. He swung toward her, sending her stress level soaring. The children, she reminded herself. She would fight anyone to protect her children's security.

"You've done a nice job with this place."

His opening words, when they came, were so mundane that she blinked.

"Thank you. We had to do a lot to make it livable."

She glanced around, wondering how her home looked through his eyes. Shabby, probably. He wouldn't see the love she'd put into this place.

She'd been so delighted to have a home of her own, after years of following her army-officer father from one post to another. No amount of work to make the apartment livable had seemed too much. She had scrubbed the wide pine planks of the floors, added inexpensive rag rugs and bright pillows to the bedrooms. This had become the kind of home she'd always longed for—permanent, filled with love and laughter and prayer.

Matt would only see how cheap it all looked in comparison to the Caldwell mansion.

He glanced around again, as if assessing the value of the furniture or noting the titles of the books on her shelves. "I suspect Harvey Gaylord didn't think much about interior decoration." Matt's face softened when he spoke of the paper's former owner. "As long as he had his books and his pipe, he was satisfied."

"Did you know him well?" This sounded like a casual conversation with a neighbor. It wasn't. It was a fencing match with the man who had the power to change her life.

"As well as anyone did. I worked for him all through high school."

"I suppose that's how you got into journalism. He was your mentor."

He smiled at the term. "The bug bit me then, not that Harvey ever let me actually write anything. I was a gofer, nothing more."

"Still, he must have been proud of your success when he turned on the television and saw you reporting from China or Taiwan or Indonesia."

Some emotion crossed his face at her casual words, so quickly, she almost couldn't identify it. Then she recognized it. Pain—pain so intense it wrenched her heart. What did rich, successful Matt Caldwell have to agonize over?

"I suppose so." His voice turned colorless, the betraying expression wiped from his face as if it had never been.

But she'd seen it, and that emotion changed the pattern between them in a way she didn't understand.

He took a breath, as if mentally changing gears. "I wanted to say again how sorry I am about your husband's death."

"Thank you." He'd sent flowers, she remembered, after Peter's accident. He'd undoubtedly heard about it from his family.

The Caldwells knew what everyone else on the island knew, that Peter Reed had skidded into a culvert on a flooded road coming back from Charleston. They didn't know what she'd found out later—that he'd never taken out the insurance he'd said he would, that his death had left his wife and children with nothing to support them but the newspaper.

"I realize you hadn't anticipated my wanting to help run the paper." Matt seemed to be picking his way carefully through the words. "Maybe I should have written to you about it."

"Maybe you should have." At least then she'd have been prepared.

Matt's face tightened, the sun lines deepening around his eyes. "That wouldn't have changed anything."

No, it wouldn't. She couldn't change the past. She'd have to find a way to cope.

She tried to block out her awareness of Matt. He stood too close to her, and his intensity seemed to reach across the inches between them. She knew what he was waiting for. He wanted her to admit that he had the right to do this.

He moved impatiently. "I assume you've looked over your copy of the contract."

"Yes, of course."

He lifted an eyebrow. "And?"

She didn't have a choice. "And I agree. If you want to help run the paper…" The words seemed to stick in her throat. What would it be like, working with Matt every day? Being forced to get his approval every step of the way?

She forced herself to go on. "I guess we're partners."

* * *

"I don't think I'll ever understand females."

Matt watched his niece run across the lawn at Gran's house toward the picnic table. A moment ago she'd been grumbling at the thought of the Sunday picnic at her great-grandmother's. Now she couldn't wait to find her cousin.

Adam, Matt's brother, smiled. "As far as I can tell, Jennifer is nine going on twenty. Nobody can understand that, especially a father." For an instant a shadow crossed Adam's face, and Matt knew he was thinking about his late wife.

The shadow disappeared as quickly as it had come. "Or did you mean your new partner?"

Matt shrugged. "Her, too, I guess. I was ready to get busy at the paper on Friday, but Sarah insisted we wait until Monday."

He'd wanted to get started. Maybe then he'd be able to erase the sense that this enforced time away from his career branded him a failure.

"Sarah's a good friend of Miranda," Adam said. "Go easy. You don't want to start another family feud."

Adam didn't say the obvious—that the Caldwell family already had to deal with a feud between their father and their uncle. Even now, their father was at one end of the crowd gathered on Gran's lawn, and Uncle Clayton was at the other.

Jefferson Caldwell, with his mane of white hair and

expensively tailored clothes, looked like what he was: a successful businessman. And Uncle Clayton—well, Uncle Clayton was an island fisherman at heart.

Matt shifted restlessly, not liking the reminder of the difference between his father and the rest of the clan. "You think I could skip the picnic? I'm not feeling very sociable."

Adam grinned. "Only if you want to take on Gran."

Naomi Caldwell marched toward them, still as erect at eighty as most people half her age.

"'Bout time you got here, Matthew."

Matt bent to kiss her cheek, inhaling the scent of lily of the valley that surrounded her. "Yes, ma'am."

Adam kissed her other cheek. "What about me?"

Gran swatted him affectionately. "You go help your cousins put up another table, heah?"

"We'll need more than one." Adam headed off.

"Adam's right." Matt glanced at the throng gathered under the trees. "Looks like you invited half the town."

"Folks want to welcome you home." Gran fixed him with a challenging stare. "You tell me, Matthew James Caldwell. Why weren't you in church this morning?"

"Still a little jet-lagged, Gran." He had a feeling that excuse wouldn't work with her.

"Nonsense. You should have been to worship."

His muscles tightened. *You should have been to*

worship. That's how Gran would see it, of course. If he told her that the endless parade of tragedies he'd witnessed had soured his soul, had made him rail at God for allowing them, she'd probably have the same answer. *You should have been to worship.* Naomi Caldwell hadn't found anything in her life that wasn't made better by turning to God.

She hasn't seen what you have, a voice whispered in his ear. She doesn't understand.

He couldn't hurt her by arguing with her about it. He gave her a quick hug. "Next week. I promise."

She patted his cheek. "Whatever brought you home, God can help."

Before he could react, she'd turned away. "I'd best see about that crab boil. You go visit with folks."

"Yes, ma'am." The crowd shifted, and he saw the one person he hadn't expected to find at his grandmother's house. "You invited Sarah Reed."

"'Course I did. She's your new partner." Gran gave him a searching look. "Something wrong with that?"

"No, Gran, nothing wrong with that."

In fact, everything was right with that. Getting better acquainted with Sarah was just what he needed. He watched her, realizing he liked looking at the smooth grace of her movements. Her hair was loose on her shoulders, tumbling in curls touched gold by the sun.

Sarah turned from saying something to Andi, and

he could sense the exact moment she spotted him. Her expressive face went still, and her hand froze in mid-gesture.

He might want to get to know her, but he suspected Sarah had entirely different feelings about that.

Sarah's breath caught at the sight of Matt's tall, lean figure. She'd known she'd see him at the picnic, of course. She just hadn't known that it would jangle her nerves so badly. He looked very tall, smiling down at his tiny grandmother. Then he looked across the lawn, and their eyes met. For an instant it was as if no one else was there.

She bent to set Amy on the grass, letting the movement hide her face for a moment. She couldn't panic at the sight of the man, for pity's sake. And she couldn't run away, any more than she could have skipped the picnic.

Amy toddled a few steps, then plopped down and started pulling grass by the handful. Sarah caught the baby's hand. "No eating grass, sweetheart."

Miranda ran to give her a hug. "You made it." Miranda, the single mother of a son about Andi's age, had become a good friend.

"I wouldn't miss it."

They joined a group of women arranging food on the long picnic table. And what food—mounds of creamy potato salad, bowls heaped with chilled shrimp, crocks of steaming chowder. The Caldwells certainly knew how to throw a picnic.

By the time the crowd had worked its way through eight kinds of pie and several gallons of coffee, Sarah had begun to relax. She'd be able to go home soon, and she'd managed to avoid saying more than hello to Matt. She rose from her lawn chair to look for the children, turned around and nearly walked into him.

She stumbled, and he clasped her hand to steady her. The warmth from his grip seemed to flow up her arm.

Nerves, she chided herself.

"Sarah. I've been hoping to talk with you." The polished voice she'd heard on television had slipped into something slower and warmer, as if he'd put his professional voice away and donned instead his comfortable, sea island tone.

"I should check on the children," she said quickly, drawing her hand away from his.

"They're fine. And we need to talk." He smiled as he said it. Anyone watching them would see only a friendly conversation. But she felt the strength that emanated from him, demanding she agree.

"The children..." she began.

"Gran's just starting to tell stories. You don't want to deny your youngsters the chance to hear a real island storyteller."

She couldn't argue with that. Her three older ones had joined the cluster of children around Naomi Caldwell, and Amy slept peacefully on a blanket with several other babies.

Matt nudged her arm. "Have a look at Gran's flowers with me."

She didn't want to go anywhere with him. She was too aware of him next to her, too conscious of his aura of coiled strength. All of Caldwell Island didn't seem big enough to get away from him.

"Fine." She summoned up a smile. "Show me your grandmother's flowers."

They strolled across the grass, toward the flower border against the white fence that separated Matt's grandmother's yard from the churchyard beyond.

Matt nodded toward the white frame cottage. "Did you know Gran's house is one of the oldest on the island? She's lived here next to the church since she married my grandfather."

Sarah couldn't help contrasting that with her own family; no one had stayed in one place for more than a year or two. But Matt didn't need to know that. "Your family has deep roots here."

"The deepest." He nodded toward the circle of children around his grandmother. "She's telling the family legend now, about the first Caldwell—a shipwrecked sailor who was saved by an island girl." His face softened as he watched the storytelling. "She's been telling it as long as I can remember, and it never changes. 'He took one look at her and knew he'd love her forever.' That's what she always says."

His words struck a chord, vibrating into her heart. Was that how love was supposed to be? If so, maybe some people were born incapable of it.

She shook the thought off, watching the group clustered around Matt's grandmother. Everyone, not just the children, was intent on the story—their story. It was part of them, and they were part of it. She hadn't felt like such an outsider since she'd come to the island.

"Is the story true?" She glanced at Matt, and he shrugged.

"Their names are in the chapel registry, and they're buried in the graveyard. The wooden dolphin he carved for her stood in the sanctuary for years. And Caldwells have been here ever since."

They'd been here ever since. The words echoed in Sarah's mind. Matt Caldwell belonged here—

But he'd chosen to go away.

The thought stuck in her head, and she was almost afraid to look at it too closely. He'd gone away. He'd built a name for himself out in the wide world. Maybe Matt Caldwell was as much a wanderer as that shipwrecked-sailor ancestor of his must have been.

She glanced up at him, wondering. Was that really the face of a man who'd settle down in a backwater town to run a weekly paper, where the most exciting story in the last month had been the theft of a shrimp net?

No. She knew a wanderer when she saw one. After

all, most of her life had been spent with a father who moved from one army base to the next with as little concern as most people would spend on changing a shirt.

Maybe she didn't have to battle Matt over who would control the paper. She could just wait him out. Sooner or later, probably in weeks, not months, he'd tire of this quiet life, and he'd be on his way. If she saw him again, it would be on her television screen.

That should make her happy. It did make her happy. She assured herself of that fact. Matt would go away, and she could go back to life as it had been before he'd walked through her door.

Chapter Three

Sarah glanced again at the children. Miranda's father had brought out a fiddle, and her brother David was leading the children in a song. Apparently the Caldwells were good at devising their own entertainment.

She and Matt stood near the flower beds that overflowed the border along the fence.

"Your grandmother must have a green thumb." Anyone watching them would think they had nothing more on their minds than the flowers.

"Gran's good at a lot of things. Flowers, needlework, quilting…and like I said, she's a born storyteller."

"Maybe that's where your journalistic talents originated."

Her comment seemed to take him by surprise, and the corners of his eyes crinkled with amusement.

"I'm not sure that would please Gran. She doesn't like the places my career has taken me."

"You're here now. That must make her happy." She held her breath, waiting for him to admit he probably wouldn't be here long.

The amusement wiped from his face. "Yes." His mouth clamped shut on the word, chilling her. Obviously he didn't intend to confide in her.

She sought for something else to keep the conversation going. "You mentioned the dolphin in the chapel. I've never seen it."

"It disappeared one summer night, years ago." The lines deepened in his face, as if he mourned the loss of that symbol.

"No one knows what happened to it?"

"No."

"Sounds like the sort of story a reporter might have tried to investigate in his younger days."

He frowned, as if he hadn't considered that. "I suppose I might have, but I never did. I guess I looked farther from home for my stories."

"Maybe you were born to be a wanderer." She held her breath, wondering what he'd say to that.

"Maybe so." Again she had the sense that this wasn't something he'd talk about with her.

Their steps had taken them around the corner of the house. Matt gestured to the flower beds that ran along the sheltered side of the building. "Gran's roses. Nobody on the island has any to compare."

"They're beautiful." Sarah touched a pale yellow rose with an apricot center, inhaling its rich perfume. "What's her secret?"

"No one knows."

His hand encircled hers, touching the rose. She felt a jolt that traveled up her arm, warming her skin. Her breath caught, and she snatched her hand away, feeling as if her cheeks were on fire.

That hadn't happened. It hadn't. She couldn't possibly be attracted to anyone. That part of her life had ended with her husband's death. She had her children, and that was enough of a life for her.

And if she were going to be attracted to someone, it certainly couldn't be Matt Caldwell, of all people.

Sarah Reed had to be the most frustrating woman he'd ever met. Matt rode along the beach early Monday morning. He'd expected to be at the office first thing, but Sarah had said that since she always worked late getting the paper out on Friday, she didn't start until ten on Mondays.

So he'd decided on an early-morning ride, hoping the horse's pounding hooves and the sea breeze in his face would clear his mind and let him approach the situation with Sarah rationally.

That didn't seem to be working. Instead of hard beige sand and blue water, he saw Sarah's face when they'd stood talking by the roses. One minute they'd been communicating, and he'd begun to believe they'd find a way of working together that would satisfy both of them. The next minute she'd turned away, gathered her kids together and left.

The pounding of Eagle's hooves echoed the pounding in his head. Nothing about his return was going as smoothly as he'd anticipated.

He'd managed to forget, when he was far away, how much the breach between his father and the rest of the family bothered him. And he'd managed to ignore the fact that taking up his partnership at the paper was bound to bring on a new set of problems. Of course, if he'd had a choice, he wouldn't have come back.

But he hadn't had a choice. *You'll take a leave of absence,* his boss had said. *Six months at least. That's the best I can do. When you're over this and ready to come back, I'll find a place for you if I can. Meanwhile, try to forget.*

The trouble was, he couldn't forget. Every time he closed his eyes, he saw himself running toward the mission station. He heard the blast, saw the walls collapsing inward, felt the concussion throw him to the ground. He'd struggled to his feet, knowing he had to help get the children out, knowing James was in there someplace.

James had been. They'd found him under a collapsed wall.

How could You let that happen, God? How? James was serving You, and You let him die.

He yanked the reins, and Eagle tossed his head in protest. "Sorry, boy." He patted the horse's neck. "Sorry."

He'd nearly broken down on the air. That was the unforgivable thing, as far as the network was concerned. He couldn't go back, not until he knew that wouldn't happen again.

Matt slowed the horse to a gentle jog. Running the newspaper would help him get himself together. It would prove to him that he was himself again—the detached journalist who didn't let personal feelings get in the way of a story. So that meant he and Sarah had to find a way of working together that satisfied both of them.

And he'd have a chance to talk to her about it, sooner than either of them had expected, probably. A small group walked along the edge of the surf ahead of him, and the morning sunlight picked out gold highlights in Sarah's light brown hair. Sarah and her kids.

Good. They could start over and have a simple, businesslike conversation. There was absolutely no reason for the unexpected wave of pleasure he felt at the sight of her.

He slowed Eagle to a walk as they approached. Sarah looked up, shielding her eyes against the sun with her hand. He couldn't see her expression.

"Sarah." He stopped and slid from Eagle's back. "Hi, kids."

"Is he yours?" Andi's eyes were huge. "Is that horse yours?"

He had to smile at her excitement. "Yes, he's mine. I don't get much chance to ride him anymore, but he's mine."

The child took a step closer, and he realized she was quivering with excitement. "What's his name?"

"Eagle. Because he can run like the wind when he wants to." He caught a sudden movement from the corner of his eye and saw Ethan dart toward Eagle's haunches. He shot his hand out to grab the boy's shirt. "Don't do that!"

He sensed Sarah's instant flare of resentment at his tone and felt an answering irritation. He was only trying to keep her kid safe. But Ethan looked scared, and he patted the boy's shoulder.

"You don't want to run up to the horse's hindquarters when he doesn't see you." He ruffled the boy's hair. "He might think you're a horsefly and kick at you."

"I'm lots bigger than a horsefly." Skepticism filled the kid's eyes.

"Well, you still don't want to startle him." Matt took out the bag of carrots he'd stuffed in his jacket pocket. "If you do just what I say, I'll let the three of you feed him a treat."

"Me first." Ethan jumped up and down.

Matt smiled at Andi. "I think Andi's first, if she wants to be."

She nodded, apparently speechless, and held out her hand.

"Keep your hand flat and let him eat the carrot," he cautioned. "You don't want him to mistake your finger for something to eat." He half expected Sarah to object, but when he looked at her, she was smiling, almost as if she approved of him.

Andi stood very straight, holding her palm out. Joy filled her small face as Eagle's lips moved against her hand. "It tickles," she breathed. "I think he likes me."

"I think he does," Matt said gently.

He looked over the child's head at Sarah. Her smile lingered, and she had a dimple in her cheek in the same place Andi did. She looked gentle. Vulnerable.

Something twisted inside him. That was what came of having a family. It made you vulnerable, put demands on you to keep them safe in an unsafe world.

He wouldn't put himself in that position—he'd figured that out somewhere in the middle of reporting an endless stream of tragedy. He wouldn't take on the responsibility of a wife or kids.

But in a way, he'd let himself in for a share of responsibility for Sarah and her little family. He didn't like the idea, but he couldn't escape it. Somehow he and Sarah had to make this work.

Sarah watched Matt. When she'd seen him riding toward them, her first instinct had been to hurry the kids up the path. Somehow she'd been caught, mesmerized by his effortless control of the huge animal. It was as if he and the horse were one.

Now he was so easily making one of Andi's dreams come true. She should say something, thank him for this....

Amy, clutching her mother's skirt for balance, toddled a few wobbly steps carrying her sand pail. She sat down abruptly on a well-padded bottom and emptied the sand over Matt's polished boots.

Would she ever have an encounter with this man when something embarrassing didn't happen? She bent to scoop the baby up, but Matt reached her first.

"Hey, little girl." His smile looked strained, but his voice was gentle as he handed her back the bucket. "Why don't you dig some more?"

"So she can empty it on you?"

Matt rose, shaking the sand from his boots. "No problem," he said easily.

"Can I give the horse a carrot now? Please?" Ethan tugged at Matt's sleeve.

Jeffrey hovered a step behind his brother. "Me, too. Me, too."

Sarah put her hands on Jeffrey's shoulders. "That's his favorite phrase, I'm afraid."

"I had a big brother, too, you know." Matt shook carrots out of the bag for each boy. "I probably said that a lot."

He smoothed Ethan's hand out. "Remember what I told Andi. Keep your palm flat."

"I remember." Ethan smiled up at him with a sudden display of trust that startled Sarah. "So he doesn't eat my finger. I'm not scared."

"Good. You shouldn't be scared of Eagle, just cautious. He wouldn't want to hurt you, but he's a big animal."

She didn't seem to be needed in this activity. Sarah sat down on the sand next to Amy, watching as Matt let her kids feed and pet the horse. He probably hadn't been around children much—he seemed to talk to them as if they were small adults—but his gentleness surprised her. *Gentle* wasn't a term she'd necessarily associate with the hard-driving reporter she knew he must be.

Finally Matt led the animal a few feet away and dropped the reins on the ground. "Eagle is ground-tied." His firm gaze touched each of the children. "He won't go anywhere unless someone startles him, so you need to stay away."

The three of them nodded soberly.

"Why don't you see if you can find any shells to add to our collection?" Sarah suggested. She'd feel more confident they'd obey if they were occupied.

The children scattered toward the edge of the water. Matt crossed to her, standing like a dark shadow between her and the sun. Then he dropped to the sand next to her.

"That was nice of you. I'm afraid Andi is horse-mad," Sarah said.

"I figured that out." His gaze was on the children, and his smile lingered.

Talking about Andi was certainly easier than discussing their business relationship. "She reads every horse book she can find, even the ones I think are too hard for her. You've just made her day."

"My niece, Jennifer, is the same."

She nodded. "Jennifer's in the same Sunday school class as Andi. She's such a pretty child."

Humor flickered in his eyes. "My brother's planning to have a nervous breakdown when she hits her teen years."

"Is that why you decided to come back? I mean, because of your family?" She was getting dangerously personal, but if she were ever to understand what made him tick, she'd have to.

"In part." His expression closed abruptly, as if he had no intention of letting her in. "Gran thinks Caldwells always come back to Caldwell Island. She says they can't ignore their roots. I'm not sure I buy that."

Since she'd never had any roots, she could hardly offer an opinion. It was what she hoped to find for her children in Caldwell Cove.

"Don't you find it a little dull here after what you've experienced?"

She'd thought his expression couldn't get any tauter, but it hardened to an unreadable mask.

"I found I needed to get out of the conflict zone."

Why? She knew she couldn't ask outright.

"So you're giving up network television for a small-town weekly?"

''For the present.'' He didn't look as if the thought gave him much pleasure. ''If you're thinking I'll take off again tomorrow and leave you in the lurch, I don't intend to.''

''I see.'' So much for her idea that he'd quickly tire of this and go away. But he might not know himself as well as he thought he did.

''Look, Sarah.'' Matt spoke slowly, watching the children scamper along the waves. ''I know we didn't get off to a good start. I know this has been an unpleasant surprise to you. Can't we find some way of working together without clashing?''

At least he seemed more conciliatory about the whole situation. ''What did you have in mind?'' she asked cautiously.

He lifted an eyebrow, as if wondering how she'd react. ''Suppose I become the publisher, and you continue as editor.''

''Meaning you make all the decisions? I don't think so.'' If she gave in to him that much, she'd never have a say in where the *Gazette* went. She had too much of herself invested in the paper to agree to that.

''Well, what would satisfy you?'' He looked as if, for once, he were really willing to listen to an answer.

It would satisfy me if you went back to your hotshot television job and let me run the paper.

No, she couldn't say that. But really, in spite of his protestations, how long was Matt likely to enjoy the quiet life in Caldwell Cove? He might think it was what he wanted now, but he'd soon be longing for the excitement he'd lived on for years.

If she could just hold on long enough, he'd go away. Things could go back to the way they'd been, and she wouldn't have Matt Caldwell messing up her life.

She took a deep breath. "Copublishers, coeditors."

She expected an argument. She didn't get it.

"Done," he said firmly, and held out his hand.

She blinked, hardly believing he'd agree without more argument. "Done," she agreed, her voice shaking a little on the word.

His fingers wrapped firmly around hers, and their warmth seemed to travel across her skin. Her gaze met his, almost involuntarily.

Matt's dark eyes seemed to grow even darker, and her breath caught. She couldn't breathe, let alone speak. It was as if they really looked at each other for the first time, without the lens of disagreement clouding their vision. Looked. Liked what they saw.

Oh, no. This couldn't be. She fought down a wave of panic. It was bad enough to be forced into an unwilling partnership with this man. Letting herself be attracted to him—worse, letting him know she was attracted to him—that was more than difficult.

It was just plain crazy.

Chapter Four

The bell over the office door rang for what seemed the hundredth time later that day, and Matt's jaw ached from gritting his teeth. That had to be the most annoying sound in the world.

Elton Hastings ambled to the counter, shoving his ball cap back on his balding head. He smiled at Sarah. "Hey, Miz Reed."

Matt lowered his gaze to his computer. He didn't have to watch or listen to know what happened next. He'd already seen it a dozen times or more since they'd arrived at the office from the beach.

Sarah would embark on an extended conversation, as she did with everyone who walked through the door. It didn't seem to matter whether they wanted to place an ad, complain about a story or stop a subscription—they'd end up telling Sarah Reed their life story.

He peered cautiously around the computer monitor. Sarah leaned forward, her brown hair swinging against her shoulder as she listened with apparently rapt attention to Elton recount his gallbladder woes. He'd known the pace of a small-town weekly would be different, but this was ridiculous.

It was past time the *Caldwell Cove Gazette* became a professional operation. He'd decided that the moment he walked into the office, and he hadn't changed his mind.

But he'd agreed that he and Sarah would be coeditors and copublishers. Looking back on that conversation, he wasn't sure why he'd agreed so easily. If he'd pushed, he might have been able to secure a stronger position for himself. In a similar situation, his father would have negotiated a better deal—he felt sure of that. He also felt sure that he didn't want to follow his father's example when it came to running a business.

He'd have to talk this over with Sarah. They were partners—she'd realize that meant a little give and take. He'd explain to her how much more efficiently the office would run if she didn't waste time chatting with every person who came in the door.

She said something that made Elton laugh, the sound almost rusty, as if the old man hadn't laughed in a while. Matt studied her face from behind the

shield of his monitor. There was strength in the line
of her jaw, balanced by the vulnerability of her mouth
and the soft warmth that seemed to radiate from her
face. Everything about her shouted that here was a
woman both capable and willing to take care of others.

Everyone responded to Sarah's warmth, even a
crusty old coot like Elton. Nothing wrong with that,
except that this was a place of business, not a church
social. Warmth and chatter were inappropriate here,
along with the tinkling bell and the plate of homemade cookies on the counter.

One of those cookies had mysteriously migrated to
his desk. He took a bite, tasting oatmeal, chocolate
and peanut butter. Giving out homemade cookies was
definitely not what he expected in a newspaper office.
Still, as long as he'd started the cookie, he might as
well finish it.

Elton finally sauntered out the door, standing a bit
taller than he had when he'd come in. Matt frowned
at the tinkling bell, then turned to Sarah.

She lifted an eyebrow. "What's wrong?"

"What makes you think something's wrong?"

The eyebrow arched a little higher. "Well, it might
be the way you stared at me the whole time I talked
to a customer."

"Was that what he was, a customer?" He feigned
surprise. "The way he confided in you, I thought he
was a long-lost cousin."

She swung her swivel chair around so that she faced him more fully. "You don't want me to be pleasant to the people who come in?" She made it a question.

"I think this operation could be a little more professional, that's all." It was probably inappropriate to take her to task for unprofessional behavior when he had chocolate smeared on one hand from the cookie he'd polished off. He wiped his hand. "This is a business."

He expected her to flare up at that—to remind him that she'd been running the paper without his help for some time. Instead, she tipped her head to one side, as if considering.

"What exactly did you have in mind?"

You could stop being so appealing. No, that wasn't what he meant. He'd mention the cookies, but eating one himself had undercut that argument.

"Listening to people's life stories. You didn't need to spend the last fifteen minutes hearing about Elton's gallbladder, did you?"

The corner of her mouth twitched. "It wasn't the most scintillating conversation I've ever had. But maybe Elton needed to talk."

"Then let him get a friend. Or a dog." He shoved out of his chair, too restless to sit still any longer. "And another thing—that bell."

She sent a startled glance toward the door. "What about the bell?"

"It makes this sound like a candy shop instead of a newspaper office." Two steps took him to the counter. He leaned against it, looking down into blue eyes that held a spark of amusement instead of the anger he half expected.

"You wouldn't say that if you were back in the copy room and nearly missed a paying customer because you didn't hear her."

"That would only happen if you were alone. You have a partner now, remember?"

Her wide eyes narrowed. "I'm finding it impossible to forget."

"It's not that bad, is it?" He realized he was leaning toward her, just as he'd seen Elton do, and he stiffened. He wasn't going to get drawn in by a pair of big blue eyes and a vulnerable mouth. "I think with a little effort, we can bring the *Gazette* into the twenty-first century."

She got up suddenly, the movement bringing her even closer. He caught a whiff of some light, flowery scent, and for a moment he was in a meadow instead of an office.

"Fine. You stay here and bring the paper into the twenty-first century by taking the bell off the door. I have a story to cover."

"Story? What story?"

She slung the strap of the camera bag over her shoulder. "Elton mentioned that Minnie Walters is celebrating her hundredth birthday today. That's worth a picture, don't you think?''

"It's not a step toward world peace." She probably wanted him to admit that her conversation with Elton had been worthwhile, and he wasn't about to do that.

"No, and we're not the *New York Times*. Our readers want to know when their neighbor hits the century mark." She turned toward the door, then swung back, holding out the camera. "Of course if you'd like to do it…"

"No, thanks." Clearly it would take more than one conversation to win this battle with Sarah. "You go ahead. I'm sure you'll get more out of Minnie than I would."

Her smile flashed, and it was like a burst of sunshine on a chilly day. "I don't know about that. She might be thrilled to have a man come calling."

"Not this man," he said firmly. "In our division of responsibilities, little old ladies who hit their hundredth birthdays are definitely your department."

Sarah's laughter mingled with the tinkle of the bell as she went out the door.

Well. The office seemed oddly empty without her. He wasn't sure who'd won that round, but at least she'd agreed he could remove the bell.

Fifteen minutes later he'd taken down the bell and begun leafing through a file of story ideas. The door from Sarah's apartment swung open, and her children

surged through. The teenage baby-sitter he'd met earlier followed them, carrying the baby on her hip.

"Tammy has to go," Andi announced importantly.
"Where's our mommy?"

"Go where?" He turned to the teenager, hoping he
didn't sound panic-stricken. "Their mother had to go
out. They can't stay here."

"I'm awfully sorry, Mr. Caldwell." She dumped
the baby unceremoniously into his unwilling arms.
"But my mama called, and she needs me to go home
'cause she has to work late."

"But the kids…"

She was already at the door. "They'll be fine 'til
Miz Reed gets back. Just watch out for the baby—
she's teething."

Watch out for the baby? She made the kid sound
like a ticking bomb. "I can't. You'll have to stay."

He was talking to a closed door. He'd been left
alone with Sarah's kids.

This was definitely not the way he'd planned to run
this office. He looked at the tot in his arms, and she
stared back at him, round blue eyes full of innocence.

He sat, balancing her on his knee, and turned to
the other three. They looked a bit more doubtful about
the situation than the baby did.

What on earth did he know about watching kids?
How could Sarah let him get stuck like this?

"Well." He cleared his throat. He'd interviewed
the leaders of angry mobs, questioned arrogant ty-

rants. He could surely talk to little kids. Just treat them as if they were responsible adults, and they'd respond that way. "Your mother will be back soon. Maybe you can amuse yourselves until she gets back."

"What can we do?" Andi asked.

"I want to play with the computer," Ethan said.

Jeffrey's face clouded up, and he looked as if tears were imminent. "I want Mommy."

Matt glanced at the baby, to discover that she was chewing on the strap of his wristwatch. When he tried to disengage her teeth, she started to wail.

Sarah, where are you?

Sarah hurried down the street toward the office, the camera bag bouncing against her hip. She'd been longer than she'd intended, but the elderly woman had been so thrilled with the whole idea of being in the paper that Sarah hadn't had the heart to cut the interview short. Besides, Minnie's tales of Caldwell Island in the early years of the century, before there'd even been a bridge to the mainland, were just what the *Caldwell Cove Gazette* readers loved.

Matt probably wouldn't agree. His determined face formed in her mind's eye, dark eyes serious, chiseled mouth firm. Her pulse gave an erratic little flutter. Maybe she needed another lecture to herself.

Matt clearly intended to keep their relationship businesslike. She must, too. He'd stay detached; she'd stay detached. She'd wait him out, and before long he'd grow tired of Caldwell Cove and the *Gazette* and take his disturbing self right out of her life.

She pushed the office door open. The first thing she noticed was that the bell was missing. The second was her children, busy enveloping Matt's desk in a sheet of newsprint.

"What—what's going on here?"

Matt straightened. He held Amy in one arm, and she was chewing on a plastic tape dispenser. "What does it look like? We're building a fort."

She was almost afraid to ask why. "But where's Tammy?"

"Gone. Something about her mother having to work late." His look was accusing. Clearly he thought she should have anticipated that and made other arrangements. Well, he was right. She should have.

Matt shifted Amy to his other arm, and the side of the fort he'd been holding collapsed, leading to a muffled shriek from Andi.

"You have to hold it." Andi peeked out from under the desk. "Or I can't stick the tape on right."

"Never mind that." Sarah hustled to the desk, hauling children out from beneath it. "You shouldn't be in here bothering Mr. Caldwell."

"We weren't bothering him," Andi protested.

"He was watching us," Ethan said.

Watching them. Their first day of working together and already she owed him a major apology.

"He doesn't need to watch you now. I'm home." She headed the three of them toward the door. "Andi, you take your brothers to the kitchen and get their snack. I'll be back to check on you in a few minutes."

"But, Mommy…"

"No buts." She marched them to the door. "Go on, now."

When they'd gone, she turned to apologize, only to realize that Matt still held the baby.

"I'm sorry." She scooped Amy into her arms, sure her cheeks must be fiery. "This shouldn't have happened. I don't know how to apologize."

Relieved of the baby, he brushed his sleeves back into place. "We seem to have survived," he said dryly. "But I hope this isn't going to become a habit."

"Of course not." Apparently he couldn't accept her apology without lecturing.

"You need adequate child care if you're going to run the paper."

She suppressed the urge to tell him she'd been running the paper and her family quite nicely without advice from him. "I have adequate child care. I just should have talked to Tammy about what to do if she had to leave."

She plopped Amy into the play yard, removing the

tape dispenser and substituting a squeaky toy before the baby could cry at being deprived of it.

"Bait and switch," Matt said.

She blinked. "What?"

He nodded toward the toy Amy had just stuffed into her mouth, and she grinned at him around it. "I tried to take the tape dispenser away, but she wouldn't give it up. You did a nice move substituting that toy." He lifted an eyebrow. "Come to think of it, that's what you did with me."

"I don't know what you mean." She was probably blushing again.

"I think you know perfectly well." He frowned, the momentary ease between them gone.

She recognized the reason for the frown. Matt had a passion for truth. She'd only known him for a couple of days, but she'd already seen glimpses of that quality. Here was a man who didn't recognize the polite little fictions most people accepted just to get through the day.

Well, she did. Sometimes perfect truth was unnecessary, even hurtful, whether Matt realized it or not. "When did I pull a bait-and-switch on you?"

"When you gave in on the bell to distract me from other things."

Other things, like cutting down on the time she spent talking to people. She took a breath, trying to phrase her concern in a way he'd understand. Trying not to sound annoyed.

"Maybe that's true. If it is, I'm sorry. I just don't know how to change the way I relate to people. And I'm not sure I'm ready to try."

She expected him to take up that challenge. Instead, he studied her for a long moment. His determined gaze almost seemed to touch her skin.

"Fair enough," he said, surprising her. "We can fight about it if we have to. Just don't try to manipulate me, even if you think it's for my own good."

She lifted an eyebrow. "Nothing but honesty?"

"Nothing but."

For some reason she thought of Peter, with his smiling charm, telling people what they wanted to hear. Matt Caldwell would certainly never be guilty of that. He was far more likely to tell you bluntly the last thing you wanted to hear.

She put the thought away for later consideration. "All right. I promise I won't try to manipulate you, even if you need it. Satisfied?"

The slightest hint of a smile quirked the corner of his mouth. "For the moment."

He retreated to his desk, and she sank down in her chair. Her heart pounded as if she'd been running a race. Maybe she had. If so, she'd probably lost.

The image brought Saint Paul's words to mind. "Casting aside all that hinders me, I run the race that is set before me." That passage never failed to spark her determination.

I know the race I have to run, Father. I have to

*love and protect and provide for the children You've
given me. Please show me the way through any ob-
stacles caused by this partnership with Matt.*

Slowly her heartbeat returned to normal. She could
do this. No matter how difficult, she'd find a way to
make this partnership work, because her children's
future depended upon it.

For the next hour she and Matt worked in the same
room, the quiet only disrupted by the two trips she
made back to the apartment to solve disputes among
the children. Amy fell asleep in her play yard. Slowly
Sarah began to relax. This wasn't so bad, was it?

"Hey, Sarah. You're looking lovely today. What
happened to your bell?"

Jason Sanders stood gazing at the doorframe, as if
searching for the missing bell.

"We decided to take it down." She carefully
avoided looking at Matt, although surely he wouldn't
object to her chatting with Sanders. The man owned
the only real-estate agency on the island, and he was
a big advertiser. "What can I do for you?"

"I really just stopped in to welcome Matt back
home." He advanced on Matt, hand outstretched.
"It's great to have the famous correspondent back
among us."

Matt stood, facing him, and she thought she'd
never seen two men so opposite. Jason was the orig-
inal glad-hander: quick with a smile, a handshake, a
compliment. It was only after she'd known him for a

while that she'd realized how facile that smile was, how trite the compliment. He seemed to have a stock of them that he rotated routinely.

As for Matt—nothing facile or charming about him, that was for sure. She studied him while the men exchanged small talk. He was always guarded, but he seemed even more so with Sanders. He stood stiffly, fists planted on his desk, expression shielded.

What did Matt have against Sanders? When the man finally waved his way back out the door, spreading a few more compliments along the way, she suspected she was about to find out.

Matt swung toward her, his stare inimical. "What was he doing here?"

"You heard him. He came to welcome you home."

He snorted. "The day Jason Sanders welcomes me anywhere is the day it snows in July."

"I take it you don't like him." That appeared to be putting it mildly. "But it must be years since you've had anything to do with him."

"Sanders was always a bully. I don't suppose his nature has changed all that much, even though he's got a better facade now."

She blinked. He'd put his finger on exactly what bothered her most about Sanders—the sense that underneath his charming manner lurked someone who always got what he wanted, no matter what it did to others.

"He's a big advertiser," she pointed out.

Matt closed the gap that separated them, planted his fists on her desk and leaned toward her. "Is that all that counts?"

Her pulse jumped. He was too close—so close she could count the fine lines at the corners of his eyes, almost feel the pulse that beat at his temple, almost touch the corded muscles of his forearms.

"N-no. Of course not." She took a steadying breath and tried to pretend he was someone else—old Elton Hastings, for example.

"Well, then, why do we have to put up with him?"

Pretending Matt was a bald seventy-year-old didn't seem to be working.

"We put up with him because our job is producing a newspaper," she said as evenly as she could manage. "It's not our job to pass judgment on our readers or our advertisers. Not unless we're running a tabloid instead of a newspaper."

She saw that hit home.

"Are you saying I'm letting my personal feelings get in the way of my professionalism?" His reluctant smile was even more disturbing than his glare had been.

Speaking of personal feelings, her own seemed to be running amok. "You told me to tell you the truth."

He winced. "Touché. That'll teach me." He squeezed her shoulder, his hand firm and warm. "Thanks, partner."

The warmth from his hand traveled all the way to

her throat, trapping her voice. She swallowed. "Anytime."

Anytime now would be the time to get over this, she lectured herself. Like now, for instance.

Unfortunately, she suspected it would take more than a lecture to neutralize the effect Matt Caldwell had on her.

Chapter Five

He didn't have any excuse for being at Sarah's apartment a few nights later. Matt paused outside the back entrance to the newspaper building, the one that led to Sarah's home, not the office. What exactly was he doing here?

He shifted the folder he was carrying. Of course he had a reason to be here—a business reason. He'd compiled a list of suggestions he wanted to talk to Sarah about, and the endless interruptions during the day made that impossible. It had nothing whatsoever to do with wanting to see her again.

Repeating that to himself, he knocked on the door. He frowned, then knocked again. Noises from inside assured him someone was home.

He glimpsed movement through the small pane at the top of the door, and finally the door swung open.

Sarah stood there, her sky-blue shirt speckled with darker spots of water. Her brown hair, also damp, curled wildly around her face.

Amy, wrapped in a towel, was equally wet. At the sight of him, she babbled something incomprehensible and lunged for him.

Sarah caught her in midlunge with the ease of long practice. "No, Amy, no. He doesn't want to hold you. You're as wet and slippery as a dolphin."

"And as pretty." Relax, he told himself. Relax. He smiled at the baby, getting an enchanting grin in return. "I'm sorry. I guess I've come at a bad time."

Sarah blew a soft brown curl out of her face. "I've never figured out how getting a baby clean can make Mommy such a mess. But, no, it's not any worse than any other time. What can I do for you?" Her tone made it clear office hours were over.

"Sorry," he repeated, feeling irrationally annoyed that he was getting off on the wrong foot with her. Again. "I thought we might be able to talk about some ideas I have for the *Gazette.* I forgot you'd be busy with the children. I can come back later."

"It's bedtime," she pointed out, probably thinking any idiot would know that. "But if you care to wait, we can talk once I get the children settled."

He suspected only courtesy had compelled that offer, but decided he'd take it at face value. It might be the only way he'd achieve his objective.

"That's fine." He stepped into the small living room. "I'll wait."

He thought Sarah suppressed a sigh as she closed the door. She nodded toward the sofa.

"Make yourself comfortable." Before he could sit down, she'd whisked out of sight, trailing the pink bath towel.

Matt turned toward the sofa. Three pairs of blue eyes surveyed him. Andi was curled up in a shabby armchair with a book. The two boys had blocks and toy cars spread across the carpet. They all looked at him.

Loosen up, his brother's voice echoed in his mind. Adam had been amused when he'd told him about being left with Sarah's kids one afternoon. *They're little kids, not the enemy. Just relax with them.*

He'd try, because this seemed the only route to the discussion he wanted to have with Sarah. He squatted down on the rug next to Ethan.

"Building a racetrack?"

The boy nodded. "It's going to be the longest one ever. Want to help?"

He tossed his folder onto the coffee table and sat on the floor. The carpet felt thin beneath him. "Hand me a couple of blocks."

Their track led across the floor, under the side table, around the armchair. Ethan kept up a constant stream of chatter, most of it telling Jeffrey what to do.

Matt had to smile. His memory provided a picture

of himself and Adam at about the same age, relating in the same way. Adam had always acted the big brother.

Andi looked up from her book now and then to watch them, and from somewhere in the back he could hear Sarah singing to the baby. This should have felt uncomfortable, but it didn't. Maybe he was getting the hang of relating to kids.

"Look out, here comes my race car." Ethan grabbed a car and sent it speeding along the track. It hit an unevenly placed block and flew off, crashing.

Matt picked up the car. "Went off track that time. Why don't you give it another try?"

"It hit a culvert," Ethan said firmly. "It's wrecked too bad to try again."

Almost before he had a chance to think it odd that Ethan knew the word *culvert,* Andi slammed her book down. "Don't say that!" she shouted. "Don't you say that!"

"Will if I want to!" Ethan shouted back.

The peaceful little playtime had disintegrated before his eyes. So much for his idea that he could relate to Sarah's children—not that he wanted to anyway. But he could hardly keep a safe distance when he was right in the middle of the battle.

"Hey, take it easy. It's okay." He touched Andi's arm, but she jerked away from him.

The tears streaking down her cheeks shocked him. Then he realized what was going on. It wasn't okay.

The cars, the wreck, the culvert—that was how their father died. It hit Matt like a fist in the stomach.

He wanted nothing so much as to get up and walk right out the door. This wasn't his concern. It was Sarah's problem. It was everything he'd come home to avoid.

But no matter how he justified it, he couldn't get up and walk away.

"I'm sorry," he said quietly, holding out his hand to Andi. "Ethan didn't mean it."

He looked at Ethan. For a moment the boy stared back rebelliously, but then he nodded. "I didn't mean it, Andi-pandy. I'm sorry."

Andi scrubbed the tears from her face with both hands. "Daddy's in heaven now," she said with a little quaver in her voice. She looked at Matt. "Did you know that?"

He suppressed the doubts that haunted his dreams. This wasn't the place to let them out. "Yes." His stomach twisted. "I'm sure he is."

"Time to put the racetrack away, boys." Sarah stood in the doorway. Her voice sounded calm, but he could tell by the strain around her eyes that she'd heard some of the conversation.

Perhaps cowed by their sister's tears, the two boys made no argument. Matt slid into a chair and tried to be inconspicuous while they hustled around, throwing cars and blocks into a plastic bin. In a few minutes the room had been cleared of toys.

"Good job." Sarah managed a smile for her kids. "I'll just be another few minutes," she informed Matt. She didn't even try to smile at him. She shepherded the children toward their rooms, leaving him alone to try and regain control of whatever was left of his mission.

The minutes ticked by. He heard soft voices from the bedrooms, realized Sarah was hearing their prayers. The gentle murmur was oddly soothing, as was the shabby room. It had a warmth that the Caldwell mansion had never achieved.

By the time he heard Sarah's step in the hall, he knew he had to address the situation with the kids before he could possibly bring up business.

"I'm sorry," he said before she could speak. "I don't know if that was my fault or not, but I'm sorry."

Sarah shook her head, sinking down into the chair Andi had vacated. "It wasn't your fault. The children come out with something about Peter's death every once in a while, usually when I'm least expecting it."

"That must be hard." He leaned toward her, wanting to say something soothing, but not knowing what it could be.

She nodded, resting her head against the chair, lids flickering closed. For the first time he noted the smudged violet shadows under her eyes, saw the lines of tiredness that she usually concealed.

She'd lost her husband less than a year ago, he

reminded himself. She was raising four children all
alone, and as far as he could tell, she didn't have any
family to help or support her. He thought briefly of
his own sprawling clan. Whether he wanted them to
be or not, they were always there.

Sarah opened her eyes, straightening as if that momentary lapse had been a failure. "We do all right,"
she said with a firmness that had to be assumed.

"I'd forgotten."

Her blue gaze darted to his face. "Forgotten
what?"

"That tragedy and loss aren't confined to war
zones." His mouth twisted. "They even happen here
in Caldwell Cove."

The words were out before he realized how they'd
sound. For a moment he thought he'd hurt her. Then
she nodded slowly.

"True enough." She got up. "I think we could
both use a cup of coffee before we talk business."

He started to protest that he didn't need any coffee,
then realized she probably needed an excuse to have
a moment alone. The way she hurried toward the
kitchen and swung the door shut behind her confirmed
that.

He took a deep breath, trying to relax taut muscles.
How exactly had this happened? He'd come here tonight to talk business with Sarah. Instead he'd seen
deeper into her heart than he had any right to. And

he'd exposed more of himself than he'd ever intended.

Sarah leaned against the kitchen counter, staring absently at the coffeepot, seeing only Matt's tense face and the battle in his dark eyes over that flare-up of emotion with Andi. Something was wrong with him. She didn't know how she knew it, but she did. Something had happened to put the strain in his eyes.

Something on the job? She ran up against a blank wall of ignorance. She'd never really thought about how they did their jobs, those people she saw on the news every night. Had Matt run into some problem out there in his other life that had carved those deep lines in his face, that had put up the barricades that screamed *Don't touch me?*

Her hands felt cold as she mechanically filled the pot with water and put coffee into the filter. Something—what had he said? *Tragedy and loss.* Had he lost someone he cared about? Was that what had brought him home?

She didn't want to know. She didn't have a right to know. But he was hurting, and she couldn't just ignore that.

Show me what to do, Lord. Is this a burden I'm supposed to pick up?

One thing was clear. Knowing why he'd come back could help her understand how long he intended to

stay. From a purely selfish point of view, she wanted
to know that.

*I'm sorry, Lord. I don't mean to be selfish. I just
can't help thinking about how Matt's actions affect
my children's future. It's not wrong to worry about
that, is it?*

She didn't have an answer by the time the coffee
was ready. She arranged cups on a wooden tray,
straightened her shoulders and went back to the living
room.

Matt sat on the sofa where she'd left him. The
folder he'd carried in with him lay, apparently forgotten, on the side table.

"Cream or sugar?" she asked as she placed the
tray on the coffee table.

"Black, please."

The routine of pouring out the coffee and handing
it to him soothed her. She glanced at his face, still
brooding, and knew she had to try and understand
what drove this enigmatic partner of hers.

She stared down at her own cup, as if it might hold
an answer. Maybe there was no way to do this but to
dive right in.

"Was that why you came back?" She suspected
she didn't need to explain. His words probably still
hovered in his mind as they did in hers. "Because
you'd seen too much tragedy?"

His long fingers curved around the cup, as if seeking heat in spite of the warm summer evening. "That was part of it." His guarded tone warned her off.

"I suppose…" She felt her way carefully. "I suppose correspondents in dangerous places have to be like doctors. They have to stay detached in order to do their jobs."

He clutched the cup so tightly she thought it would shatter. "That's what's supposed to happen. Sometimes it doesn't work that way. When you're in the middle of a fight, innocent bystanders can get hurt."

Her gaze flew to his face. "Were you injured?"

"Not physically." A muscle twitched in his jaw, the only sign of the iron control he must be exercising. "Let's say I lost my detachment for a while. I started to burn out."

"So you decided to come home." To heal? That was what she suspected, but she thought he'd reject the idea. She also suspected he wasn't telling her all of it. Why should he? They were virtual strangers, linked together by circumstance.

"I decided—we decided, my boss and I—that I needed a break. I took a leave of absence."

"A leave of absence? That means you intend to go back. You didn't tell me that."

He set the cup down with a little clatter, and his eyes met hers. "No, I didn't tell you. I guess I should have."

"I thought you meant to stay for good." She grappled to get her mind around this new idea. He'd never intended to stay at the *Gazette* for the long haul. Knowing that to begin with could have saved her some agonizing. "What happened to partners telling each other the truth?"

That might have been a shade of embarrassment in his expression. "All right, you've got me. Maybe I'm a little too used to answering only to myself. I should have been up-front about my plans."

Yes, you should have. "Why don't you start now? How long is this leave of absence of yours supposed to last?"

"Six months." He said it as if it were something to cling to. "Six months of peace and quiet. Then I go back."

"What if you're not ready in six months?"

Anger flared for an instant. "I'll be ready. I'll go back."

Her own anger sparked. "So working at the *Gazette* was just something to amuse you while you're on leave."

"I'm not looking for amusement," he snapped. He shook his hand then, held up his hand as if to stop whatever she might say to that. "I'm sorry. I realize this doesn't make much sense to you."

"Explain it to me. You walk into our lives and turn them upside down, and then you tell me it's just temporary? You're right, it doesn't make much sense to me."

Whatever had been conciliatory in his expression fled. "I own a half share in the paper, remember? If I want to help run it for six days or six weeks or six months, I can."

She felt suddenly tired. He was right. He could do whatever he wanted, and she couldn't stop him.

"Sarah, this doesn't have to be a problem. Being a part of running the paper will let me keep my hand in my profession while I'm off. What would you expect me to do? Help my grandmother prune her roses for six months?"

Her mouth curved in a reluctant smile. "No, somehow I don't see you as the rose-pruning type."

His face relaxed a fraction. "You must see that this was the obvious solution for me. And it can be a break for you, too."

"What do you mean? I can't take six months off."

"No. But you could take a few hours a day off, with my help. You can't tell me you wouldn't welcome that."

"You mean I can work twelve-hour days, instead of fourteen?" She said it lightly, but somehow it didn't come out that way. If she ever admitted how tired she was, she might collapse and never get up again.

"Something like that." His gaze searched her face. "We share the work for six months, right? We both gain. At the end of that time, when I go back, we can look for some extra help for you."

She wanted to protest that they couldn't afford extra help, but maybe that was an argument better saved for another day. She'd wanted to know what brought Matt home, wanted to know how long he'd stay. Now she had both of those answers. It should make her happy.

It did make her happy, she assured herself. She had to put up with Matt's interference at the paper for six months, and then he'd be gone. She could go back to handling things the way she wanted to. Surely she could deal with anything for six months.

"Well, I guess that's settled, then."

"I guess it is." Matt glanced around, as if he were searching for something he'd forgotten. Maybe he just wanted something to get them away from the dangerously personal ground they'd been treading.

He reached for the folder he'd brought with him.

"Your plan of action?" She raised an eyebrow.

"Suggestions," he said firmly. "Ideas I have for the paper." He held it out to her. "Take a look and tell me what you think."

She took the folder gingerly.

"It won't bite." His mouth curved in a smile.

Won't it? She opened the manila cover with a sense of inevitability. Whatever Matt proposed, it meant change, and none of the changes she'd endured recently had been pleasant.

She read through the pages, schooling her face to

impassivity. She hadn't quite finished when Matt put his hand impatiently on hers, making her pulse jump.

"Well, what do you think?"

"You have some interesting ideas," she said carefully. "But I'm not convinced some of these will work for *Gazette* readers."

"Why not?" He shot the question at her.

She suspected the brief interlude of peace between them was over. "You have to realize people want different things from a small-town paper than they do from a television news program."

He was already shaking his head. "Oh, I know you have to do the local stuff. People expect that. But there's no reason why the *Gazette* can't cover more important issues, as well. After all, things that happen at the state and national level affect all of us."

"But, Matt…"

His hands clasped both of her wrists, sending their warmth straight to her heart. For the first time, she saw his face as it must have looked before stress and tragedy had left their mark on him—alive with passion and enthusiasm. "There are stories waiting to be told here in Caldwell Cove, Sarah. Let's take a crack at telling them, all right?"

She knew he wasn't really asking for her permission. He'd found the road he wanted to travel, and no one would deter him, least of all her.

She swallowed hard, trying to slow the race of her

pulses. Matt would only be in her life for the next six months. But in six months, he could do irreparable damage to the newspaper.

And if she weren't careful to guard against it, he could also do irreparable damage to her heart.

Chapter Six

"How are you surviving with your new partner?"

The question fit so exactly into Sarah's thoughts that it startled her. She turned to smile at Miranda Caldwell, letting a tidal wave of Sunday school children scurry past them to the tables in the churchyard. The church coffee hour had been moved out under the trees on this beautiful June Sabbath.

"Fine, I think." She suppressed all the worries she couldn't express to anyone, and especially not to Matt's cousin. "Maybe you should ask him that question."

Miranda's smile broadened. "I did. And he said, 'Fine, I think,' just like you did, sugar. Seems the two of you think alike."

Sarah's gaze rested on Matt's tall figure as he stood

beneath a tree, balancing a coffee cup and talking to his brother. "I don't think I'd say that, exactly."

"Then what?" Miranda nudged her arm, her green eyes alight with mischief. "You can tell me. We're family, Matt and I."

And that was just why she couldn't. Did Matt's family recognize the strain implicit in the stiffness of his shoulders? Did they see the despair she sometimes glimpsed in his eyes? Or was she imagining the whole thing?

She had to respond to Miranda in some way. "Let's just say Matt takes more of a world view toward a small-town paper than I do."

"Crusading, is he?"

Sarah thought of the stories Matt had proposed over the course of the last week. "Yes, I guess you could say that. He has good ideas. Just maybe not sensible for us to tackle."

"That's Matthew. He's always been a crusader." Miranda smiled in reminiscence. "I remember when we were kids. He was always the one who took on the schoolyard bully. Never to defend himself—always to defend somebody smaller or weaker. That's our Matt."

She hadn't viewed Matt that way, but it fit. "The *Gazette* isn't exactly the schoolyard." And Jason Sanders, even now handshaking his way around the coffee hour, wasn't the bully Matt apparently remembered.

"Maybe you need to tell him that," Miranda said. She nodded. "Seems like you're about to have the chance."

Sarah looked up to see Matt bearing down on them, moving with the determined stride that said he had important things to do.

"See you later," Miranda murmured, and slipped away before Sarah could suggest that she stay.

It wasn't that she needed a barrier against her new partner. It was just that Matt was sure to ask what she thought of the article he'd written about Jason Sanders's acquisition of small parcels of land from some elderly island natives. And if she told him what she thought, it would lead to a quarrel she didn't want to have, at least not on Sunday morning.

"Good morning, Sarah. Nice service, wasn't it?"

"Very nice." Did he really think that? He hadn't been in church the previous Sunday, and she thought she'd detected an extra measure of tension when her gaze had strayed toward him during the service. Maybe he'd been looking at the empty bracket where the Caldwell dolphin had once stood. Caldwells must be reminded of the story and the missing dolphin each time they went into St. Andrews.

"Gran got after me for sleeping in last Sunday." Matt seemed to be reading her mind. "She doesn't accept excuses for missing worship."

"If you're looking for sympathy, you've come to the wrong person," she said firmly. "I have four kids to get ready, and I still managed to get everyone here for Sunday school."

His face relaxed in a smile, and he held up both hands as if to fend her off. "Okay, I surrender. No sympathy here." He glanced toward the group of children playing tag under the trees, while three teenagers corralled the nursery toddlers on a blanket. "At least you get a break once you bring them here."

"The nursery helpers are good with the children. I just wish I could find someone reliable to watch them during the week when I'm working. Tammy's good with them, but she's not available often enough."

That was a constant concern, and she hadn't been able to take seriously Matt's contention that she could take time off now that he was working with her. Getting the paper out provided more than enough work for both of them. Matt was a fast learner, but he came in knowing little of the everyday mechanics of getting the paper out.

So far, Matt hadn't complained about her children playing hide-and-seek under his desk, but she suspected that was just a matter of time.

"Speaking of work, what did you think of the article I asked you to read?"

It had taken even less time than she'd expected for him to bring up the prickly subject.

"I thought it was interesting. Well written."

His eyes narrowed. "That means you didn't like it."

"I didn't say that. It just raised some concerns in my mind, that's all." Such as whether they'd lose their biggest advertiser if Matt printed that story.

"I went over the piece with a microscope," he said stiffly. "I can assure you there's nothing in it but the truth. He's been pressuring people to sell who don't know the potential value of their property."

"But it's the truth told as bluntly as possible." They were at war again, this time at a church coffee hour, of all places. "You could have softened it. But maybe you didn't want to. Maybe you were fighting the schoolyard bully again."

"You've been talking to Miranda." His gaze shot sparks, but his voice was soft.

She met his look defiantly. "How can you be sure you're not letting your history with him affect your decision?"

"I don't know, Sarah. How can you be sure you're not letting his advertising dollars affect yours?"

Anger stiffened her spine. "Advertising is what keeps a weekly paper alive. I have to be concerned about that. You don't."

He looked surprised by the direct attack. "What do you mean? I'm just as interested in the paper's success as you are."

The worries she'd bottled up all week seemed to be spilling out in a most inappropriate place. "You can't be," she said flatly. "To you, the paper is just something to keep you busy for the next six months, until you go back to your real life.''

''I care about the *Gazette*. Maybe you think I'm not committed—''

''Committed? Tell me something, Matt. Where's your passport?''

It didn't take the betraying movement of his hand toward his jacket pocket to tell her what she'd already guessed. He wouldn't put that passport away, because it was a lifeline to the world he wanted.

''This is just a temporary aberration in your life. But for me, for my family—''

''Miz Reed?''

She blinked, so intent on making Matt see that for an instant she couldn't refocus. Then she saw the girl leading Jeffrey by the hand.

She was on her knees next to him immediately. ''Sweetheart, what is it?'' She brushed fine blond hair back from his flushed face. ''Don't you feel okay?''

He shook his head, leaning against her. ''My head hurts, Mommy. And my tummy doesn't feel too good.''

She picked him up, straightening. ''We'll go home right away.'' She glanced at Matt, but he was looking at Jeffrey.

''That's too bad, buddy.'' He put his hand on Jeffrey's forehead.

It was the simplest gesture, one she'd made herself more times than she could count. But the sight of the man's strong hand, gentle on her son's head, made her heart clench.

She pushed the feeling away. She'd analyze it later. "I'd better round up the other kids."

"Let me." Matt frowned. "Better yet, let me bring the older kids home later. They're happy playing for now. That way you can get the little ones settled."

"I can't impose—"

"It's not an imposition." His smile wiped away all trace of their quarrel. He took Jeffrey from her. "I'll carry him to the car while you get the baby and settle the other two."

She should be annoyed at his assumption of responsibility. She'd been handling her family on her own for quite some time. But it felt so tempting to let Matt bear a little of the burden, just for now.

She shouldn't give in to that feeling. Matt would be gone soon. She shouldn't let him become so entangled with her family. But she couldn't seem to help it.

"Here we are, kids." Matt pulled up at Sarah's door. He'd been relieved to finally leave the church with them. He'd found it hard, as long as he was at St. Andrews, to keep his eyes from straying toward the stained-glass window of Jesus blessing the children. He didn't want to look at it, but for some reason it tugged at him.

He opened the car door for Andi and Ethan, wondering if he could just dump them and make his escape. Unfortunately, being back on the island seemed to reactivate all the Southern manners that had been drilled into him since birth. The answer was no, he couldn't. He had to go in and speak to Sarah, at least.

He would have knocked, but Andi already had the door open when he reached it. He was surprised to see Sarah apparently ready to go out.

"What's going on?"

She looked harried. "I can't get Jeffrey's fever down. I'm going to run him over to the clinic." She managed a distracted smile. "Thanks for your help. Andi and Ethan, let's get in the car."

"But, Mommy—"

"No arguments, please." She had Jeffrey in one arm and Amy in the other. "Just bring my bag, Andi."

"I'll watch them." The words were out of his mouth before he realized it, and part of him stood back and watched, appalled, as he reached out to take the baby from her.

"I can manage." Sarah clutched Amy.

She was clearly just as reluctant to let him as he was to do it. Somehow that made him more determined.

"Don't be silly." He pried the baby out of her arms. "You need to concentrate on taking care of Jeffrey."

An image of the children he hadn't been able to

help flickered through his mind, and he buried it. He wouldn't let Sarah's kids remind him of that.

"If you're sure—"

"I'm sure." He pushed her gently toward the car. "We'll be fine until you get back. If there's anything I need to know about the baby, Andi will tell me."

Jeffrey gave a little sob and burrowed his head into Sarah's neck. She stroked his hair gently.

"It's all right, sweetheart. The doctor will make you better." Her gaze met Matt's. "Thank you," she said softly.

The door closed behind her. Amy wailed and lunged toward it. With a convulsive movement, Matt caught her before she lunged right out of his arms. His heart pounding erratically, he set her down. She'd be safer on the floor. If she got hurt while he was watching her… The images came again, and this time it took more effort to oust them.

Amy wailed for another moment, then grasped the chair and pulled herself up to stand, holding on, wobbling a little. Apparently her storm was over.

He looked at Andi and Ethan. "You have to tell me, guys. What are we supposed to do now?"

"Watch television," Ethan began. "And then—"

"We change out of our church clothes first," Andi said firmly. "Then we have peanut-butter-and-jelly sandwiches, and we play quietly while Amy takes a nap."

Looked as if Andi was the one to count on. "Okay,

let's do that.'' This shouldn't be too difficult. Anyone could make peanut-butter-and-jelly sandwiches and put a baby down for a nap.

An hour later he decided he'd been overly optimistic. The sandwiches had gone fine, although Andi pointed out that Mommy always cut them in triangles, not rectangles. And Andi and Ethan were, indeed, playing relatively quietly. But Amy didn't want to take a nap.

Frustrated and helpless at her wails, he lifted her back out of the crib and sat down in the cushioned rocker next to it. He could picture Sarah in the sunny nursery, rocking and singing.

"Come on, little girl." He patted Amy's back, and her cries reverberated in his head. "Give me a break."

He tried to think. What would Miz Becky, the Gullah woman who'd raised him and Adam after their mother died, have done in a situation like this?

A fragment of memory slipped through his mind. He seemed to feel warm, comforting arms rocking him back and forth while a rich Southern voice sang.

He may as well give it a try. Nothing else seemed to work. He rocked. "'Hush, little baby, don't say a word—'"

What came next? He couldn't remember, but then it came back to him. He hummed the bits he didn't remember, rocking in time to the song. Amy's wails diminished, then ceased. It became a game, trying to remember the verses, hearing Miz Becky's voice in his mind. It seemed to comfort him as much as it did the child.

By the time he'd remembered all the words to all the verses, Amy was asleep on his shoulder. He watched her, feeling a kind of wonderment. She was so relaxed and trusting, deep into slumber. He could see the fine tracing of blue veins under rose-petal skin, the soft crescents formed by her eyelashes against her cheeks.

He expected the moment to be shattered by his nightmare images of wounded, hungry children, but it wasn't. He could only feel…what? He sought for the word. *Blessed,* that was it. He could only feel blessed to share this peace.

Andi tiptoed into the room, clutching a book, and inspected the sleeping baby. "You can put her in the crib now," she whispered. "She's asleep."

"I know." He smiled. "I'm afraid she'll wake up if I move."

"Just hold her close against you." Andi adjusted his hands. "And then put her right down. That's what Mommy does."

"If it's good enough for Mommy, I guess it's good enough for me." *Please don't let me wake her.*

It was only after he'd put the baby safely into the crib that he realized that was the first time he'd prayed without anger for a long time.

He and Andi tiptoed back out of the nursery.

"Thanks, Andi. You were a big help." He noticed the cover of her book. "That looks like a good horse story."

She nodded. "I wanted to ask you something." She opened the book to the place she'd been holding with one small finger. "See what it says here? About using a pick to clean the horse's foot?" Her blue eyes were anxious. "Doesn't that hurt the horse?"

"Not at all." He put his hand on her shoulder, surprised by the fragility of her small bones. "The horse doesn't have feeling in that part of his hoof. But if a stone got caught under there and he walked on it, that would hurt."

He could almost see her process that. "It's like my fingernails," she said.

"Exactly." He felt an irrational pride at her swift intelligence. "Maybe you can come over to my house one day, and I'll show you how to do it."

Andi's breath caught, and she clutched the book against her chest. She looked as if he'd promised her the moon. "Could I really?"

He was probably offering something he'd later regret, but at the moment it seemed worth it. "Sure." He squeezed her shoulder. "We'll do that."

She skipped out to the living room, probably to tell Ethan about the promised treat. He followed more slowly, wondering at himself. He wasn't going to get involved with Sarah and her kids—wasn't that what he'd told himself? He didn't seem able to keep that promise, and he wasn't quite sure why.

By the time Matt heard Sarah at the door, he'd finished a rough draft of his editorial and played three games of Chutes and Ladders with Andi and Ethan.

"How's Jeffrey?" Matt got up to close the door for her as she carried him in.

"Feeling better, I think. The doctor says it's a virus that's going around. I just hope everyone doesn't catch it."

He couldn't help but notice the tired shadows under Sarah's eyes as she stroked Jeffrey's silky hair, and he felt a surprising, unwelcome wave of protectiveness. He wanted to wipe her exhausted look away, but he couldn't.

"Do you want me to carry him to bed?"

"I'll just let him rest on the sofa for now." She lowered the child to the corner of the sofa and tucked an afghan around him. "Okay?"

Jeffrey nodded, his eyes drifting shut.

She turned to Andi and Ethan. "Why don't you go outside and play for a bit, okay? I'll call you when Jeffrey wakes up."

When they'd gone, she smiled at the game board spread out on the coffee table. "I hope they weren't boring you to tears with that game."

"Actually, I learned quite a lot this afternoon." He started to put the pieces back in the box, but found he was watching Sarah instead. "I learned the rules of Chutes and Ladders, I learned I really do remember all the verses to 'Hush, Little Baby' and I learned that Andi is the most responsible little girl I've ever met."

"Too responsible, I'm afraid."

Sarah sat and leaned back in a chair, brushing a strand of hair away from her face. He could almost feel the silkiness of it against his own fingers.

"Was she always that way?" He didn't want to bring up her husband's death, but he wondered.

"She was a caretaker from the moment she was born, I think."

"Like her mother."

She looked at him with faint surprise. "Is that how you see me?"

"Definitely." He might not understand everything about Sarah, but that he knew. "You're like Miranda—always taking care of everyone."

She smiled. "Whether they want it or not." Faint worry lines showed between her brows. "Andi's been worse since her daddy died. I wish I could convince her she can just be a little girl."

He thought of his niece. Jennifer was nearly a year older than Andi, but in some ways she seemed younger—certainly more carefree. Well, why wouldn't she? She'd lost her mother, but she had family who'd take care of her no matter what.

"Too bad I can't give you a little of my excess family."

Sarah looked startled for a moment, and then she seemed to follow his train of thought. "I guess my children are a little lacking in that department. No cousins, no aunts and uncles…"

"No grandparents?" He ventured the question.

Sorrow touched her face. "I'm afraid they just have me."

"I'm sorry."

She nodded in recognition of his sympathy, then seemed to turn away from it. "What about Ethan? Did you learn anything about him this afternoon?"

He thought he detected wariness in the question. "I learned he doesn't like to lose at Chutes and Ladders." He wasn't about to say that he'd caught the child in a clumsy attempt to cheat.

"Yes." The shadow in her eyes told him she understood what he didn't say. "Ethan does like to win. Well, most children are like that at his age. He's just very competitive." Defensiveness threaded her voice.

"He has a lot of charm." He put the lid on the box. "Reminds me of your husband."

Her mouth tightened. "Peter was always charming." She said it as if he'd implied an insult.

"Nothing wrong with that." What was going on behind those big blue eyes? Was there something about Peter Reed he should know?

"No, there's not." She stood up abruptly and held out her hand. "Thank you, Matt. I appreciate your help today. It was very kind of you."

Apparently he was expected to leave. Well, that was what he wanted, wasn't it?

He took her hand, feeling the warmth that seemed to flow from her every touch. "It was a pleasure," he said formally. "I like your kids, Sarah." To his surprise, he realized it was true.

And something else was true, something he wasn't about to say. He liked Sarah Reed, too. Maybe a little bit too much.

Chapter Seven

"Looks pretty good, doesn't it?" Matt unfolded the fresh issue of the *Gazette* on Friday morning, feeling a ridiculous surge of pride. He leaned against Sarah's desk, willing her to agree with him that the first issue he'd had much input on had turned out well.

Sarah nodded. "Not bad for a small-town weekly. And there's your name on the masthead."

"So it is." He couldn't seem to prevent a smile.

She tilted back in her swivel chair. The blue shirt she wore made her eyes even bluer. "Come on now. You've been featured on the television news. You're not going to tell me the *Caldwell Cove Gazette* holds a candle to that."

"Well, I have to confess it's the first time I've covered the important story of the garden club's annual awards night."

"Not big enough?" Her voice was gently teasing. "It's important to people in Caldwell Cove. They want to know who won the award for the best roses. Oh, let me see." She pretended to consult the story. "That happens to be your grandmother."

"I told you no one could grow better roses than Gran." The smile lingered on his mouth. A couple of things surprised him about this day. One was the pride he felt in his first issue of the paper. The other was the pleasure his new relationship with Sarah engendered.

He looked cautiously at that. Things had changed between them during the last week. It wasn't just the fact that he'd helped on Sunday when she'd needed it.

They'd grown closer to each other. He hadn't intended that, but it had happened.

You're just getting used to having her around, he told himself. That's all. There's nothing more to it than that.

Used to having her around, used to having the kids around. He glanced over at Amy, contentedly chewing on a teething ring in her play yard. The little imp had been steadily working her way into his heart, and he couldn't seem to prevent it.

The other kids were back in the apartment, watched by yet another in the string of teenage baby-sitters Sarah had to rely on. Jeffrey seemed to have recovered from his bug. Matt could hear his voice raised in protest about something.

Sarah was reading through the front page, frowning a little. Looking for errors, he supposed. He'd learned, getting this issue of the *Gazette* out, that she was a perfectionist.

He'd learned a few other things, too. His gaze traced the soft line of her cheek, her straight nose, her stubborn chin. In just over a week he'd discovered Sarah's particular combination of strength and nurturing.

The warmth that made her reach out to every person who came through the door no longer seemed annoying, as it had that first day. It was as much a part of her as her attention to detail and her swift intelligence.

If he were honest with himself, he'd admit that he couldn't ignore the attraction he felt for her. He'd sensed it the day they met, and being around her every day had made it grow stronger. He didn't intend to act on it, of course. That would be unthinkable.

Except that he was thinking about it, especially at moments like this, when he stood close enough to smell the light, flowery scent she wore, close enough to see the smallest change in her expression.

As if in response to his thought, her expression did change. A slight frown creased her brows, and he knew she was reading the story he'd done on Jason Sanders.

"You still don't like it, do you?" He didn't need to explain what he meant. She'd know.

"It's not a question of like." She seemed to pick the words out carefully. "You did a good job of reporting the story."

Her caution annoyed him. Or maybe he was more annoyed at the fact that she questioned his judgment.

"You still think I made a mistake in running it."

"I'm just worried about repercussions." She shook her head, forcing a smile. "Forget it. I worry too much. I'd better start setting up the ads for next week's issue."

She turned to her desk, as if dismissing the question. The trouble was, he knew she hadn't dismissed it, not entirely.

She'd gone along with his decision to run the story. That was the important thing. There was no point in beating the subject to death.

Returning to his desk, he opened the file of projected feature stories. Maybe he ought to take on something a bit less controversial for next week's issue.

He was mulling over the possibilities when the phone rang. He heard Sarah's cheerful answer, then heard the way the happiness drained from her voice.

He swung to look at her. She pressed the receiver to her ear, and a wave of brown hair flowed over it.

"I'm sorry to hear that." Her tone was carefully

contained. "Is there anything I can do to change your mind about this decision?"

She paused, listening. He found he was listening, too, as if he could hear the voice on the other end of the line.

"No, I'm afraid we can't. I'm sorry you feel that way about it."

Sarah winced, as if the caller had slammed the phone down in her ear. She returned the receiver gently to the cradle.

"What is it?" He was afraid he knew.

"Jason Sanders." She looked at him, her face expressionless. "He's just withdrawn all his advertising from the *Gazette*."

He stood. What was there to say? "You warned me this might happen."

She grimaced. "Oddly enough, I'm not taking too much pleasure in being right."

"Look, Sarah, this isn't so bad. We can do without Sanders's advertising. It won't make or break us."

Sarah pushed her hair back from her forehead, as if it had gotten heavy. "Maybe not," she said noncommittally.

"Running the story was the right thing to do. We can't pick and choose our stories based on our advertisers." He hated the fact that he sounded defensive. "We're going to be all right. You'll see. We'll pick up more readers."

"Readers don't pay the bills. Subscribers and advertisers do. That's the reality of a weekly paper."

"Then we'll get more advertisers." Was he trying to convince her or himself?

"I hope so." She pressed her hands flat against the desk, as if to ground herself. "Whether we do or not—" Her expression seemed to harden. "I agreed to this partnership. I'll take the consequences."

He wanted to argue, wanted to protest that he was right in this. He didn't doubt that. He was right.

Unfortunately he wasn't the one with the most to lose from this decision. Sarah was.

She was beginning to read Matt too well. Sarah bent over the folder of community calendar events, but her gaze was on Matt. He'd been quiet since that morning's call, but she could almost sense what he was thinking.

He felt regret, she was sure of that—regret that he'd caused problems for her by his actions. But he didn't regret writing the story. It wasn't in him to turn back from doing what he thought was right.

She suppressed a sigh. That might be a very admirable quality, but it wasn't an easy one to live with.

Not that she ever anticipated doing such a thing, she assured herself hurriedly. But she had to work closely with him, and the result was the same.

She studied Matt's face, straight dark brows drawn down over his eyes as he worked. He gripped a pencil with his right hand, turning it over and over in his fingers.

She had to push down the warmth that resulted every time she looked at him too closely. She had some regrets of her own over this situation. She regretted the loss of the comradeship she'd begun to feel with him since Sunday. But she certainly wasn't foolish enough to think there ever could be anything else.

Amy began to fuss, shaking the rail of the play yard. Sarah started to get up, but Matt beat her to it.

"I'll get her." He jerked a nod toward the folder he'd been looking through. "I'm not making much progress anyway."

He lifted the baby, holding her close against his cheek for a moment, and Sarah's heart lurched. Did Matt even realize how much he'd bonded with Amy since Sunday? And if he did, would it make a difference?

She already knew the answer to that question. Nothing would turn him back from doing what he thought was right. She could only hope he wouldn't find any other advertisers to antagonize.

"She's really close to walking." He bent over, putting her down on her feet, holding Amy's tiny hands in his large ones, and she toddled a few proud steps.

"Amy's a little later at that than the others were." She'd much rather talk with him about Amy than about business. "I think it's because she's always been such a placid baby. She didn't feel the need to get going as soon as they did. Andi in particular.'' She smiled reminiscently. "She was only ten months when she took her first step. I remember Peter said—" She stopped abruptly.

"What did he say?" Matt prompted.

She didn't talk much about Peter, but this was a happy memory. "He thought she'd end up being a track star because she moved so fast."

"Maybe she will. Caldwell Cove High could certainly use one."

"Maybe." If they were still here when Andi was ready for high school. If the paper survived, so that she could afford to stay here. If—too many ifs.

I want to stay, Lord. I want to put down roots here for my children. Please show me the way to make that happen.

Was that a selfish prayer? She should probably be asking God to show her the right path, instead of being so sure she already knew it. But surely He wouldn't have given her such a strong need to make her home here unless it was in His plan.

Matt chuckled. Amy had let go with one hand and stood wobbling, trying to reach out to the rung of his chair with the other.

"Take it easy, little girl. I don't think you're quite ready for that yet." His voice was gentle, his face as relaxed as Sarah had ever seen it.

If he ever looked at her that way— Sarah stopped

that thought before it could go any further. She wasn't looking for romance, and certainly not with a man whose idea of settling down was six months in one place. She had the children, and that was all she could handle in her life just now.

A wail sounded from the apartment, followed by the sound of Wendy, the new sitter, calling her name.

"I'm sorry." She sent Matt an apologetic look as she started for the door. "Do you mind keeping an eye on Amy for a moment?"

"We're fine." He waved her off.

She scurried back to the apartment and settled a quarrel that a competent sitter should have been able to handle on her own. If she could only find someone really reliable to watch the children, this would be so much easier. Matt must be bothered by the constant intrusion of her family life into work, even though he didn't say anything about it.

She was on her way to the office when she heard a thump, followed by a cry from Amy and a muffled exclamation from Matt. She raced back through the door, heart pounding.

Matt clutched Amy against him, and blood dotted his shirt. His face was so white she thought him the injured one, but then she saw the cut on the baby's lip.

"She's hurt." He sounded almost frantic. "We've got to get her to the doctor."

She reached him then, taking the baby in her arms,

automatically searching for other injuries as she soothed her. "Hush, sweetheart, hush. Let Mommy see." She grabbed a clean diaper and pressed it against Amy's quivering lip as she sank down into the chair. "It's okay."

"It's my fault. I should have been watching her more closely." Matt pulled out his keys. "I'll drive you to the clinic."

"I don't think that's necessary." She cradled Amy against her. The piercing wails turned into muted sobs. "It's not a deep cut."

"But the blood—" He sounded so shaken that she looked up at him. His face was still white, his eyes filled with grief and remorse.

"Facial cuts bleed." She tried to sound matter-of-fact. "Believe me, I've rushed to the doctor more times than I care to count. This isn't bad. Look, it's nearly stopped already." She stroked Amy's cheek. "She bit it with one of those new teeth of hers. It happens."

"It was my fault," he said again.

Why was he overreacting to this? "Matt, it wasn't anybody's fault. Babies fall. She'd have fallen if I'd been watching her." She smiled, reaching out to him with one hand. "Honestly, you didn't do anything wrong."

Matt shook his head, his mouth tight. Then, before she could say anything else, he turned away. In a moment he'd gone, and she was left staring at the closed door, wondering what on earth had just happened.

She searched Amy's little face. "You okay, darling?"

Amy responded with a smile and a babble of baby talk. Sarah hugged her close.

"Sure you are." She frowned at the door. "But Matt's not."

She didn't know why, but the small incident with Amy had upset him way out of proportion to the cause. She'd thought she was beginning to know him, but maybe she was wrong. Maybe she didn't understand him at all.

He'd let himself be responsible, and a child had gotten hurt. Matt stared at his reflection in the baroque mirror that graced the center hallway of the Caldwell mansion. Guilt seemed to look back at him.

The nightmares he'd hoped were gone would be back tonight. He could be sure of that.

The doorbell chimed, interrupting his thoughts. He glanced at the grandfather clock against the wall. Nearly nine. They weren't expecting anyone tonight, as far as he knew.

He pulled the door open. Sarah stood there.

For a moment he just looked at her, caught by the way the fanlight put gold highlights in her hair. Then reality hit.

"What's wrong? Is it Amy? Was it worse than you

thought?'' A dozen frightening possibilities chased each other through his mind.

"Amy's fine.'' Sarah reached toward him with that warm reassurance he'd seen her extend to the children. "Matt, she's okay, really. Just a bit of a fat lip to show for her tumble.'' She shook her head. "It probably won't be the last one, unfortunately.''

Relief flooded him. "Then what?'' He realized how brusque that sounded. "Please, come in. I'm just surprised to see you.''

She stepped into the hallway, her sandals clicking on the black-and-white-tile floor. She'd traded the slacks she'd worn earlier for a skirt of some soft material that moved when she did. She looked around with frank curiosity.

"So this is how the other half lives.''

He grimaced. "Just a tad ostentatious, isn't it?''

Before she could make what would have to be an awkward reply to that, Jennifer came bouncing down the steps.

"Hey, Miz Sarah. Is Andi with you?''

"Andi's home getting ready for bed.'' Sarah smiled at his niece.

Jennifer pouted. "I wish you'd brought her with you. We could have played. I want to show her my new dollhouse.''

"I'm sure she'd like that,'' Sarah said gently. "Another time.''

An idea tickled his mind, and he put it away to be

considered later. "Mrs. Reed and I have to talk, Jenny-girl. I'll see you later."

When Jenny looked mutinous at being dismissed, he took Sarah's arm. "Let's go out to the veranda. It'll be quiet there."

She nodded, letting him guide her through the door. She probably thought he didn't want her in his home. That couldn't be further from the truth.

The reality was that nothing about the mansion felt like home to him any longer, if it ever had. And he had no desire to discuss business with Sarah while they chanced being interrupted by his father.

Business must have brought her here, since Amy was all right. His father already thought him crazy to have bought into such a poor investment as the *Caldwell Cove Gazette*. He'd undoubtedly have some caustic advice about holding on to advertisers, if he knew about Jason Sanders.

They walked to the end of the veranda and sat in the wicker swing, piled high with cushions, that had always been his favorite spot for thinking. Sarah's skirt draped over the print pillows as she settled.

Her gaze seemed to trace the length of the veranda, and he wondered what she thought of it all. Did she see the showplace his father wanted it to be?

"Jenny's a sweet child." Her comment, when it came, surprised him. "It was nice of her to invite Andi over."

"She's quite a little person. I feel as if I've just finally gotten to know her."

"Maybe you were never here long enough." Sarah tilted her head to look at him, and moonlight touched her face, turning it silver.

"Maybe not." Maybe he shouldn't be here now. He didn't seem to belong after all this time. "Jenny really warms up this cold house." He gestured toward the Tara-like mansion that loomed over them.

"Cold?"

He couldn't see her eyes clearly in the moonlight, but he could hear the caring in her voice. He shrugged.

"Sounds like I'm whining, doesn't it? But this house has always been more showplace than home. After our mother died, the only really comfortable spot was the kitchen. Miz Becky always made sure we had plenty of loving."

"Who was Miz Becky?" Her voice was so soft it prompted the feelings he'd often thought but seldom expressed.

"Is, not was. Miz Becky takes care of us all. She raised four kids of her own, then took on the two motherless Caldwell boys. I'm not sure what we'd have done without her." He took a deep breath, clenching his fist on his knee. "Okay, enough small talk. You can let me have it."

A frown wrinkled her brow. "What do you mean?"

"You must be unhappy to go to the trouble of hiring a sitter so you could come here tonight. I figure that means you want to speak your mind about the paper without anyone around to overhear. I caused you enough trouble today. The least I can do is take the heat."

She shook her head, her hair moving like silk. "That's not why I'm here."

He resisted the impulse to touch her. "Why then?"

"Because I'm worried about you." The caring in her voice seemed to cross the inches between them and wrap around his heart. "You really overreacted to Amy's little mishap today." She put her hand on his. "Please, Matt. Tell me. What happened to you?"

Chapter Eight

Sarah held her breath, waiting for Matt's anger to spike, waiting for him to tell her to mind her own business. Or, worse, waiting for him to laugh at her presumption.

He didn't seem to be laughing. A shaft of moonlight cast his face in light and shadow—all bone and muscle without daytime's color to soften the effect. It was a study in determination, a warrior's face.

"I don't know what you mean." He said the words stiffly, without any emphasis at all. "If that's why you've come, I'm afraid you've wasted a perfectly good baby-sitter."

She wouldn't be put off. She'd spent too much energy arguing with God about coming at all, and she'd lost.

"I don't think so." She chose her words carefully,

trying to find the ones that would unlock the riddle that was Matthew Caldwell. "I saw your face this morning when Amy was hurt."

He shrugged, but the attempt at casualness wasn't convincing. "I'm sure there are plenty of men who get queasy when they see a baby bleeding."

"Matt, that wasn't queasiness. Believe me, I've seen enough sick kids to know the difference."

"Fine, have it your way. Whatever you think you saw in me—"

He started to get up, and the swing lurched beneath her. In a moment he'd be gone.

"Grief," she said. "Overwhelming grief and remorse, just because the baby fell."

He turned toward her, the swing's chains creaking in protest at the abrupt movement. Now the anger she'd been expecting flared in his face. "All right, have it your way. I overreacted. That's all. I overreacted."

"Because of something that happened to you while you were overseas." She didn't know why she was so sure. She simply knew.

Matt's face hardened to a bleak mask. "What happened is none of your business."

At least he'd admitted that there was something. "Matt, it doesn't help to keep things bottled up inside. You need to talk about it."

His hands moved, as if pushing that away. "Trust

me, Sarah. If I felt the need to unburden myself to someone, I have plenty of family to choose from.''

Yes, he did. She had none, except the kids, so she couldn't understand what that was like.

''I know you do. Have you talked to any of them?''

''No.'' He bit off the word.

Please, Lord. You put this burden on my heart for him. You made me see I had to come here tonight. Please show me the words that will help him.

''Matt—'' She couldn't tell him she'd begun to care. She didn't want to admit that even to herself. ''I realize we haven't known each other very long. But we're partners. If something affects you, it affects me.''

''Does it?'' He almost sounded as if he wanted to believe that.

''Yes.'' She spoke firmly. He'd never know that she had feelings for him, but that didn't matter. What mattered was that he was hurting, and she wanted to help. ''Please. Tell me what's going on with you.''

''You won't like hearing it, Sarah. You might not be strong enough to hear it.''

She sensed the longing beneath his bitterness. He wanted someone to listen and to care. He couldn't ask, but he wanted that. She reached out to clasp both his hands in hers.

''Tell me.'' The words came out a little breathlessly, but not because she was afraid he'd turn back now. She could feel the current running between them through their clasped hands. They were linked in a way she didn't quite understand, as if they'd known each other a long time ago and had just come together again.

Hearing what was burdening his heart would bring them even closer, and that closeness would eventually bring her more hurt. But Matt needed her right now, probably more than he realized. She couldn't let him down.

"I haven't talked to anyone about this since I got home."

She could hear something rustle out in the marsh beyond the veranda, but Matt's need kept her attention pinned to him.

"They haven't asked?" She gripped his hands more tightly, as if she could send comfort through them. Hadn't his family seen the pain in his eyes?

He shrugged. "I think my grandmother knows something's wrong. That's why she keeps reminding me of my verse."

"Your verse?"

His mouth twisted in what might have been an attempt at a smile. "It's another one of those Caldwell family traditions, like the dolphin. We all have a Bible verse we were given when we were baptized. Gran picked them for each of her grandchildren, the way her mother and grandmother did before her."

"A family tradition." It sounded like a good, comforting thing, like the swing rocking gently under them. "What is your verse?"

"Romans 8, 28." He stopped there, as if he didn't want to say the words.

But she knew them. "'And we know that in all things, God works for the good of those who love Him, who have been called according to His purpose.'"

"That's the one."

"It's a good promise to live by," she said softly.

"That's what James used to say." His voice roughened.

He looked down at their clasped hands, and the lines in his face seemed to deepen, as if she saw him growing older right in front of her.

"James?"

"James Whitman. He ran a mission station in Indonesia. I'd known him in college, so I looked him up when I was sent there to report on the Timorese situation."

Scattered memories flickered through her mind—images of bombed streets, frightened civilians, gangs of soldiers and militia. "That was a dangerous place to be."

"James used to laugh about that. It had been so quiet since he'd arrived it was almost boring, he said. Then the political situation changed, and nothing was quiet anymore." He shook his head. "That didn't stop him. He went right on doing his job, running his school, feeding anyone who came to his door in need, even if they turned around and robbed him.''

''He sounds like a good person.''

''He was.''

Matt's grip tightened on her hands until it was painful, but she didn't pull away. She couldn't.

''I wanted to do a story on him, to showcase the good he was doing in the middle of chaos. He said no, but I kept after him. Finally he agreed. He should have kicked me out the first time I mentioned it.''

''It didn't go well?'' This had to be worse than a botched story.

''Actually the interview went very well. James was articulate, the kids were photogenic, everyone at the network was pleased.''

A night bird cried somewhere out in the marsh, and Matt jerked as if it had been a shot. She tried to soothe him with the firm clasp of her hands.

''What went wrong?''

He grimaced, as if in pain. ''Unfortunately it hadn't occurred to us that the terrorists watched television, too. The night after my report aired, I heard a rumor they planned to attack the mission station. I tried to get there to warn James and the others. I was running toward the gate when the bomb went off.''

She made an inarticulate sound of grief. His hands jerked spasmodically. He might want to stop, but he wouldn't be able to now.

''We found James and a co-worker in the rubble.

Dead.'' The words rolled out inexorably. ''Seven of the children were seriously injured. We had to dig them out. I can still hear them crying.''

Her throat was so tight it seemed impossible to speak, but she had to. ''Matt, it wasn't your fault. It was a terrible thing, but it wasn't your fault.''

''Tell that to the people who died.'' His mouth twisted bitterly.

''You couldn't have known. James must have been more familiar with the situation than you were, and he didn't suspect that would happen.''

''That doesn't make me any less guilty.'' He sounded as if he were passing judgment on himself.

''The people at the network didn't blame you, did they?''

''Blame me? No. I'm sure they regretted the bombing, but it certainly made quite a story for my next broadcast.'' His bitterness ran so bone-deep that she didn't know how it ever could be relieved.

''They didn't expect you to—''

''Report my friend's death?'' His tone mocked her. ''Of course they expected it.''

Her heart seemed to be crying. ''How could you possibly do that?''

''Not very well. I nearly broke down on the air. Funny, but that's the one thing they couldn't forgive. That's why I'm in exile. Not because I did an interview that led to a good man's death, but because I nearly broke down on the air.''

Sarah felt as if she hadn't breathed in a long time. She took a breath, steadying herself. "So you decided to take a leave of absence to get over it."

"I didn't decide. My bosses decided. 'Get a grip on yourself, Caldwell. You're no good to us like this. Go back to your island until you learn to cope out here in the real world.'"

She struggled to get her mind around that. She'd assumed that this leave of absence was his idea. Now it turned out it hadn't been. He was here under protest, trying to put himself back together.

"So you'll go back, once you've come to terms with this. Your job will be waiting for you."

She tried to sound reassuring. He'd go back. Odd, that his presence could have come to mean so much to her in such a short period of time.

"That's my life. Ugly as it can be, it's my life. I want it back." His voice roughened. "When I get it back, believe me, there won't be a repeat performance. I won't ever let myself get that close to anyone again."

Matt couldn't believe those words had come out of his mouth. Shock rippled through him. How could he be saying these things to anyone, especially to Sarah?

He'd told her things he hadn't told anyone else. Not even his brother knew the whole story behind his return. And he'd just spilled it all to a woman he'd only known a couple of weeks.

"Matt—" Sarah's voice was troubled. "You can't live detached. No one can."

"I can try." He wanted to pull his hands free of hers, wanted to cut this short and walk away.

But he couldn't. Talking to Sarah, feeling her caring, had begun to melt something that had been frozen inside him. Like thawing cold hands, it hurt, but he knew it was doing him good.

"Is that really what you want for yourself?" She shifted a little, and the swing moved beneath them as she turned toward him more fully.

He wanted to say something light, something that set them at a safe distance. But Sarah was looking at him with her generous caring heart shining in her eyes, and he couldn't do that.

"Want?" He should let go of her hands. He should get up and walk away. "I don't know that *want* is the right word. It's what I *need* to survive out there." He jerked his head toward the mainland. She'd know he meant everything out there, beyond Caldwell Island.

"Maybe you don't belong out there any longer." Her voice was so soft, he leaned closer to hear it. "Maybe your life is meant to be here."

"No. My life is waiting for me." He tried to sound sure of that. He *was* sure of that.

But the moonlight tangled in Sarah's hair, etching it with silver, and the soft lowcountry night closed around them, cradling them in its warmth. Warm—

almost as warm as Sarah, leaning toward him, longing to make him better.

"Sarah Reed." He touched her hair, feeling the springy curls wind around his fingers. "Sympathy her specialty, given to anyone and everyone, regardless of whether they deserve it or not."

"It's not a question of deserving."

"No?" He said it softly, prolonging the moment.

Her eyes, soft in the moonlight, met his. Her lips parted, as if she were about to say something, and then she seemed to forget whatever it was. He heard the soft sound of her breath, felt her hand tremble under his.

"Sarah." Her name was gentle on his lips, as gentle as she was, with her combination of softness and strength. She'd gotten under his guard in a way he'd never expected anyone would, ever again.

"Matt, I—"

He touched her cheek, smooth and sweet as the skin of a fresh peach. Stroked the line of her jaw. Cupped her chin in his hand and tilted her face toward his. Found her mouth with his.

Longing surfaced within him. He drew her closer, feeling her respond as if she, too, had been waiting for this moment. As if this kiss had been predetermined from the first time they saw each other.

Maybe it had. He held her close. Maybe it had.

Sarah drew back, too soon, with a small sound that might have been protest. He trailed a line of gentle kisses across her cheek. Sarah was everything he needed now—warmth, caring, peace. This might be a mistake, but he couldn't let her go.

"We shouldn't." Sarah breathed the words. Her hand moved against his chest to push him away, but then she clutched his shirt instead, feeling the steady beat of his heart beneath the smooth cotton.

"I know, I know." He held her close within the protective circle of his arm. He took a deep breath, as if he'd been without oxygen for too long. "This isn't a good idea."

"We're partners." She sought for all the rational arguments she knew were there, somewhere, if only she could find them.

"We have a business relationship." She thought there might be a thread of amusement under his agreement, but she didn't know if it was at her or himself. "We shouldn't mix that up with something personal."

"No, we shouldn't." She straightened her spine, pulling free of the comfort of his strong arm around her. She didn't need to lean on anyone, she reminded herself. Certainly not Matt Caldwell.

"I'll be leaving soon." He said it with certainty. He moved, withdrawing his arm, putting another inch or two between them. "You know I can't deny I'm attracted to you, Sarah. But it would be a mistake to start something that has to end. Especially where your children are concerned.''

The children. She fixed her mind on them, trying to ignore the way her heart continued to flutter at Matt's nearness.

"We agree, then. It would be too hard on the children to let them think—well, think there was something between us that's not going to be.''

There, she'd put things in perspective. Matt would understand that. Now she just had to convince her own heart, which was showing a surprisingly rebellious streak at the idea.

"We're partners," Matt said again. "Friends.''

She nodded. "Friends. That's all. Just friends.''

He clasped her hand briefly, then released it. "You helped me tonight, Sarah. I didn't know how much I needed to talk about James until you forced me into it.''

She tried to smile. "You make it sound as if I used a baseball bat.''

"No. Just a persistence and determination that would do credit to a reporter on the trail of a hot story.''

She sensed his relief that they had moved into less emotional territory. She wanted to stay there, too. It was safer. But something nagged at her, something that had to be said.

"Matt, if we are friends, will you let me give you some friendly advice?''

He nodded, but she thought he stiffened.

"When Peter died, I was angry with God." She picked the words carefully. "I thought He had let me down, leaving me alone with four kids to raise."

Matt didn't respond. Maybe he knew where she was going and didn't want to hear it. But he had to. She had to say it, because no one else would. He hadn't opened up to anyone else, so this was her responsibility.

"Eventually I realized God hadn't gone anywhere. He was right there with me, helping me every step of the way." Her voice choked in spite of her effort to keep it calm. "I wouldn't have made it without Him."

Matt nodded stiffly. "I'm glad for you, Sarah. But I—"

"You're angry with God," she said quickly, before he could finish. "You think God let you down. Let your friend down."

He swung on her then. "Didn't He? How else would you explain it? Or do you have some nice little platitude that will make the pain go away?"

His words hit her like stones, and she tried not to flinch. "No platitudes," she said softly. "Just my own experience. God was big enough to handle my anger and grief and bring me through to the other side. He's big enough to handle yours, too."

Matt got up, setting the swing rocking. He stood looking down at her, as remote as a stranger.

"I appreciate what you're trying to do, Sarah. But I'm going to have to handle this my own way."

"Are you handling it?"

"Yes." He bit off the word. "I'm handling it fine on my own."

He wasn't, but he wouldn't admit that, not yet.

"I guess there's nothing else to say but good-night, then."

Something seemed to soften his stern expression. "I didn't mean—" He stopped, shook his head. "Thank you, Sarah. I'll walk you to your car."

Their heels clicked as they walked the length of the veranda. Matt held the car door for her, then stood for a moment looking at her. He was going to say—

"Good night, Sarah." He turned away.

He didn't want God's help, didn't want her help. She started the car, and shells spun under her wheels as she pulled through the white pillars that marked the gate.

Well, Matt might not want her help, but he needed it. She'd have to go on trying. Despite whatever they felt or didn't feel for each other, she couldn't let him wall his soul off and not try to help him.

And if she succeeded? She tried to look at that steadily as she drove down the narrow street. If she helped Matt heal, she knew what would happen then. He'd go away, taking her heart with him.

Chapter Nine

He didn't know why he was so nervous about this. Matt glanced across the office at Sarah a few days later, wondering at himself. He had a simple suggestion to make, one that Sarah should welcome. So why was he acting like a teenager about to ask a girl on a first date?

The kiss, that's why, the small voice of truth murmured in his heart. You kissed her, and you haven't figured out how to deal with that.

He had dealt with it, he argued. They both had. They'd agreed that anything other than friendship between them would be a mistake. They both knew that, and they'd go on from there.

He watched the tiny lines that formed between Sarah's brows as she looked over something on her desk. That attention to detail was part of her. She brought the need to do things right to everything she touched, including her kids. Maybe that was why he hesitated to approach her on this.

No perfect words appeared in his mind. He'd better just do it.

"Sarah." He approached her desk. She glanced up and a soft brown curl caressed her cheek, momentarily distracting him.

"Is something wrong?"

"No, nothing. In fact, I have an idea that might be very helpful." He marshaled his arguments in his mind. "How would you feel about your kids spending afternoons at the house with Jenny and her babysitter?"

"The house?" She looked blank.

"My house. My brother thinks it's a great idea."

Distress crossed her face. "You're bothered by having the children around. I know this isn't a conventional way to run an office, but—"

"No, that's not it at all." He should have realized she'd jump to that conclusion. "You must know by now that I like your kids."

As soon as he said the words he realized how true they were. He hadn't intended this to happen—it certainly wasn't part of the detachment he'd been cultivating. But her children had worked their way into his heart when he wasn't looking.

"Then why are you trying to get rid of them?"

Sarah pushed her chair back, her face guarded, as if preparing for a fight.

"Look, I think we could deal with two problems at the same time here. Jenny needs playmates—there are no young families close enough to the house to make that easy. And you need a few hours a day when you're free to concentrate on the paper, instead of always wondering if the current baby-sitter is up to par."

"There's nothing wrong with my baby-sitters." She was quickly defensive. "They may be young, but—"

"But all the older kids have other summer jobs. I know. I remember what it's like." He sat on the edge of her desk, trying a smile, hoping to relax the conversation. "Every teenager on the island who wants to work can find a summer job, and baby-sitting comes at the bottom of the list."

Sarah didn't relax. "Even if that's true, I don't expect you to come to my rescue. Providing childcare is not one of your partnership responsibilities."

He lifted an eyebrow. "Are you always this prickly when someone wants to do something for you?"

"I don't like to take charity." Her clear blue eyes clouded. "I remember—" She stopped.

"You remember what?" He leaned forward, suddenly wanting to know what brought that distress to the surface. "This isn't charity, but never mind that for now. What do you remember?"

He saw the struggle in her face. She wanted to tell him; she didn't want to tell him. "Come on, Sarah. I've leveled with you. Don't I deserve the same?"

Her smile flickered briefly. "It's nothing very important."

"Then there's no reason not to tell me why that's such a hot button for you."

She shrugged. "Have it your way. My father was career army. He was posted all over the world, and since my mother died when I was a baby, I went with him."

"I didn't know that." Maybe that explained why Caldwell Cove was so important to her. She wanted a stable home for her own kids.

"I wasn't much older than Andi when we lived in Germany." She frowned. "I don't know why money was so tight, but it was. I had to have uniforms for the school there, but Dad couldn't afford them. So the headmistress called me in, and they had this big box of cast-off uniforms. The teacher went rooting through them, trying to find something that would fit. Nothing did, and Dad certainly didn't know how to alter anything." She looked down, as if seeing a too-big school uniform. "I went through that whole school year looking like a ragamuffin." She grimaced. "Silly, I know. But it made me a little touchy where accepting charity is concerned."

She'd ended on a light note, but his throat was ridiculously tight. He kept seeing the little girl she'd been, with blond pigtails like Andi's, feeling hurt and ashamed that she wasn't like the other kids.

"As I said, this isn't charity." He tried to keep his tone brisk. "At least, not for you. We want to provide a job for Miz Becky's niece, so she can earn next year's college tuition. She keeps insisting watching Jenny isn't enough work."

She smiled. "And you think watching my crew would be enough to justify hazard pay."

He smiled back, relieved that they seemed to have moved out of emotional territory. "Something like that. You can consider it helping a deserving young woman get her education. So, will you do it?"

Sarah held his gaze for a long moment, as if probing his intent. Finally she gave a hesitant nod. "I guess we can try it for a day or two."

"Fine." He got up quickly, before she could change her mind. "We'll start this afternoon."

She looked startled. "Wouldn't it be better to wait until a few days? We should give Jenny's sitter a chance to prepare."

"Wanda's ready now. And Jenny can't wait to have them there to play. We'll run them over around one. You mentioned your sitter has to leave then, so this will work out perfectly. All right?" He could feel the resistance in her.

"We'll try it," she said again. "If it's too much for the sitter—"

"It won't be," he said, inordinately pleased that

he'd pulled this off. Sarah would accept his help. She'd undoubtedly give him an argument about who paid Wanda, but he'd deal with that when it happened.

The important thing was that he could help her and, in a way, make the paper run more smoothly. He silenced the little voice whispering in his mind that this was another giant step into each other's lives.

How had she let herself be talked into this? Sarah got out of the van, looking nervously up at the pillared veranda as she took Amy out of the car seat. She couldn't feel at home in a place like this. Her kids didn't belong here. What if they broke something?

"We're ready." Matt shooed the kids toward the veranda. "Let's go find Wanda and Jenny."

At least the children didn't seem to sense her nervousness. Andi skipped along at Matt's side, perfectly confident, while the boys peppered him with questions.

Sarah tried not to let her gaze slip sideways to the swing where they'd sat Wednesday night. Where they'd kissed.

Matt held the door open, and the kids scurried inside. He gestured for her to enter.

She should have stuck with her initial no. Working with Matt every day was bad enough. Having her children in his house was worse.

There was only one solution—she'd have to find some reasonable excuse to get out of this. Clutching Amy, she crossed the threshold into the Caldwell mansion.

She stood in the wide center hallway, getting her bearings, noticing things she'd been too preoccupied to see on Wednesday night. To her right was the formal dining room, with its crystal chandelier and mahogany table and chairs carved in the rice design that was typical of the sea islands. To the left, a ceiling fan circled lazily above elegant Queen Anne furniture placed on what seemed an acre of Oriental carpet.

Ahead of her a circular staircase soared upward, looking as if Scarlett O'Hara would descend at any moment. But that wasn't Scarlett coming toward her down the steps. It was Matt's father.

Jefferson Caldwell approached with cool assurance, holding out his hand. "Ms. Reed. Welcome to Twin Oaks."

"Thank you." She shook hands, trying to assess her impressions as Caldwell turned to his son with a question. *Distinguished*—that was probably the word. That leonine mane of white hair, those piercing eyes—Jefferson Caldwell looked like a man who was used to getting what he wanted.

She glanced from him to Matt, wondering. Coolness tainted the air between them. She couldn't help but see it.

Was this because of Matt's partnership in the newspaper? If his father disapproved of that, she could hardly imagine that he'd want her children cluttering up his house.

Jefferson turned to her, looking as if his mind had already moved past her to something more important. "Miz Becky is waiting for you in the kitchen, and I expect the others are there, too. Y'all go on back. Make yourselves at home."

"Thank you." She relaxed marginally. At least Caldwell Sr. didn't seem actively opposed to their presence. But if he had been, that would have given her the perfect excuse to call this whole thing off.

"This way." Matt shepherded them through a swinging door at the end of the hallway, his step quickening.

Suddenly they were in a different world—one with linoleum underfoot, geraniums blossoming on the windowsills and a ginger cat weaving around the legs of the woman who turned to greet them.

"'Bout time you were getting back here with them, boy." Miz Becky buffeted Matt with an affectionate blow to his shoulder, but her eyes were on the children. "Y'all are welcome in my kitchen, y'heah? Andi, Ethan, Jeffrey." She greeted each of them with a gentle touch to head or cheek. "And this little darlin' is Amy."

She scooped the baby from Sarah's arms, murmuring to her softly in Gullah, the language of sea island natives. Sarah could only look on in amazement as Miz Becky charmed her children.

Matt had said she'd taken care of him and Adam after raising her own children, so Miz Becky had to be sixty, at least. But she was as proudly erect as any queen, and the glossy black hair that wrapped around her head in a kind of coronet showed not a trace of gray.

This part of the house looked different, smelled different, felt different. Where the front was all cool elegance, Miz Becky's kitchen felt warmly loving.

The biggest change was in Matt. The tension she'd sensed when he was with his father had disappeared entirely. He teased the children gently in Gullah as he helped Miz Becky carry a pitcher of lemonade and platter of molasses cookies to the back porch.

Sarah followed, wondering. What kind of home was it, when the son of the house felt more at home in the kitchen with the housekeeper?

"This is my niece, Wanda."

The tall young woman who'd been playing a game with Jenny at the porch table rose to shake her hand. "It's nice to meet you, Ms. Reed." She smiled. "And the children. Andi, Ethan, Jeffrey." Like her aunt, Wanda called them by name, but her language didn't have as much of the slurred Gullah accent. "I see Aunt Becky has already laid claim to the baby. I'll be lucky ever to get my hands on her."

"But—" Sarah looked at the woman who cradled

Amy against her cheek. "I don't want to impose on you. I'm sure you already have plenty to do running a big house like this."

"Sugar, you couldn't make me happier if you tried." She rocked Amy gently, and the baby's eyes started to close. "I've been longin' for another baby to love around here, and it started to look like that wouldn't happen."

Matt held up his hands in defense. "Hey, I've brought you Amy. You can't ask for more."

His quick words jolted her heart. No one could ask for more from Matt. She'd known that since their talk Wednesday night. His experiences had convinced him the only safe life was a detached one, and that undoubtedly extended to having a family of his own.

That was his decision. The twinge in her heart was totally uncalled for.

She still wasn't convinced that the Caldwell housekeeper should be watching her baby. Had anyone bothered to consult Jefferson Caldwell about that?

"Miz Becky, I'm just not sure—"

"Hush, child." She jerked her head toward the kitchen door. "Come in and see what we've fixed up for this little one."

Matt had joined the children and Wanda at the round table on the porch and was pouring out lemonade. She followed Miz Becky into the cool kitchen and then to a small room that adjoined it.

Becky's gesture encompassed it. "This used to be

a maid's room, but nobody lives in it anymore. Matt helped me get it ready."

Sunlight slanted through the window and lay in patches on the wide plank floor. The room had been turned into a nursery, with a crib, changing table and a box of baby toys.

"You've gone to so much trouble."

"No trouble." Miz Becky lowered Amy to the crib. The baby stirred, then slipped deeply into sleep, one hand curled against her cheek. "These things were our Jenny's when she was a baby. She was right excited to help us get them out for Amy. And Matt was the most at peace I've seen him since he got home." She smoothed one hand along the crib railing. "That boy needs a little peace. If he gets it from helping your young ones, that's not such a big thing to ask, is it?"

Sarah blinked back tears, thinking of Matt's face when he'd talked about the children he'd heard crying for help after the bombing that killed his friend. Maybe this could be a step in his healing.

"No," she said softly. "It's not a big thing to ask at all."

They walked back to the porch.

Wanda had the children lined up on the step while she laid out the house rules for them with quiet authority. "Y'all listen when I call you, stay out of the front of the house and don't run through the flower beds or my daddy will get after you. He takes care of those flowers, and he's right proud of them. All right?''

Sarah half expected Andi to argue or Ethan to try and wheedle his way out of the rules, but all three nodded solemnly.

"That's fine, then." Wanda flashed them a wide smile. "Let's have a game."

The children followed her onto the lawn, and Matt rose, moving to her side. "See?" he said. "Plenty of room for them to play safely. That's the stable, beyond the garages, with the vegetable garden beyond that."

"And that?" She pointed to the raw skeleton of a building rising behind the outbuildings.

Matt grimaced. "My father's latest project. He's putting up a few new houses on the lane behind the estate."

"Don't you like the idea of neighbors that close?" Or was it something about his father's business that bothered him?

He shrugged. "Doesn't matter to me." Implicit in it was that he'd soon be gone. "Well, Sarah?" He gave her a challenging look. "You find any flaws in our arrangements for the kids that would let you back out?"

He shouldn't be able to read her that easily. She felt a twinge of panic. How had she let him get so far into her life?

"No flaws." She managed a smile. She could be gracious about this, after all.

"Then let's get back to work."

He took her arm as he spoke, his hand warm against her skin, and her pulse jumped. Work—just the two of them in the office. Before, the children had always been nearby, forming a buffer by their presence. Now she and Matt were really going to be alone together.

"The worship is ended. Let the service begin." Pastor Wells held up his hands in benediction, and the organ burst out in joyful music.

Sarah stood still in the pew for a moment, letting the peace she'd been seeking for the last several days seep into her. St. Andrew's Chapel—its minister and its people—had been a blessing to her since the day she arrived on the island. She loved it—loved the tiny wooden sanctuary that felt almost like a boat inside, loved the ancient stained-glass windows, loved Pastor Wells's sermons, always so filled with joy.

A fragment of guilt touched her. She had to admit that she hadn't listened as closely as she should have to the day's message. Matt had been seated three rows ahead of her. She'd forced herself not to look, but even when she'd had her gaze fixed on the pulpit, awareness of him hovered at the edge of her mind.

Stop it, she lectured herself sternly. She saw more than enough of Matt all week. They probably both needed a break from each other on Sunday, especially now that the children spent afternoons at the mansion. Hopefully by the time she picked the children up from the nursery and the junior church, he'd be gone.

When she emerged into the churchyard a few minutes later, people still clustered under the trees, chatting. Before she could head toward the car, Jason Sanders broke away from a nearby group and approached her. Tension skittered along her nerves. She hadn't talked to Sanders since the day he'd withdrawn his advertising.

"Good morning, Jason." She hoped he wasn't planning to be difficult.

"Sarah, good to see you." He beamed as if she were a long-lost relative. "How's everything at the paper?"

The children, apparently considering this a reprieve from going home, scurried off to chase each other around the sprawling branches of a live oak.

"Just fine." She shifted Amy to the other arm. Sanders had to know his actions had put a dent in their budget, but she wasn't about to admit that.

He lifted an eyebrow, some of the joviality leaving his face. "Can't be easy for you, breaking in a new partner. Especially someone like Matt Caldwell."

She felt her smile freeze on her face. "Matt's doing fine."

"Still, can't be like working with Peter." He

sighed. "Terrible loss. I always liked Peter. It'd be a shame to see the paper change from his vision for it."

Her lips felt stiff, but she managed to make them move. "Nothing has changed about the *Gazette*." She glanced past him, seeing Matt approach. "Perhaps you'd like to talk with Matt about it."

"Think I'll skip that pleasure." He turned to move off, then glanced back at her. "I'd like to resume my advertising, Sarah. I surely would."

"I hope you'll think about it."

He nodded, then was gone before Matt reached her.

"What did he want?" Suspicion colored Matt's voice as he glared after Sanders.

"I'm not sure." What had been the point of that little exchange? She didn't know, but she knew it made her uneasy.

Matt shook his head, as if dismissing Sanders. "Pastor Wells has something he'd like to talk with us about."

Amy, hearing Matt's voice, made a lunge toward him. He caught her as if he'd been doing that all her life and carried her as they walked to the minister. "Tell Sarah what you were just telling me. She'll be interested."

Was that his way of palming something off on her that he didn't want to do?

Pastor Wells tickled Amy's cheek. "I was asking Matt if he realized the two-hundredth birthday of the church is coming up this year." He looked lovingly toward the frame building. "It's hard to believe, isn't it?"

"I hadn't realized. You must be planning a celebration." Somehow she had the feeling they were going to be asked to do something.

"Yes, of course. And part of that celebration should be a recognition of the role St. Andrews has played in the island's history."

She nodded cautiously, hoping that didn't mean he wanted her to write that history.

"So I thought the *Gazette* would run a series of articles." He beamed, as if he were giving them a present. "I have boxes of historic material, and I know people would want to read about it."

"I'm sure you're right, Pastor. That's exactly the sort of thing our readers love." She glanced at Matt, daring him to argue. Certainly it wasn't the sort of article he loved.

But Matt nodded. "Great idea. Let me know when the material is ready, and I'll stop by to pick it up."

"Wonderful." Pastor Wells clapped his hands together, beaming. "I'll have it ready in a day or two."

Someone else called his name then, and he moved off, still smiling.

"Admit it, Sarah." Matt lowered his voice, standing close enough that none of the other parishioners gathered on the lawn could hear. "You thought I was going to turn the poor man down."

Once again he seemed to be looking into her mind.

"I was afraid you might not find the church's birthday celebration hard-hitting enough."

"Even I know St. Andrews's bicentennial is important," he said. "Besides, how involved can it be? You'll look though the material, find some way to present it so it's not as dry as dust—"

"Hold it right there. How did this suddenly get to be my job?"

"Human-interest stuff is more your forte than mine."

"But this is your church, your town. You grew up here." She thought of the Caldwell legend and the missing dolphin that still meant so much to all of them. "You know all the old stories. I'd say that makes it yours."

A smile tugged at his lips. "Okay, ours then. We'll work on it together. Agreed?"

"Agreed."

His smile faded as he glanced across the churchyard. "I have another story I want to pursue, as well. Something that will be more hard-hitting."

She followed the direction of his gaze, and her heart sank. "You're tackling Jason Sanders again."

Matt's expression hardened. "I got a tip that there's something shady about a deal he has going at the far end of the island. I intend to look into it."

Reason told her that Sanders had already withdrawn his advertising. He couldn't do anything else to them. But a warning voice whispered in her mind that he wasn't a good enemy to make.

"Do you have to do this?" She knew before she asked the question what his answer would be.

"Of course. That's what a journalist does." He looked surprised that she could even ask. "If I could break an important story..." He let that trail off.

But she seemed to know what he was thinking. If Matt broke an important story, he'd be proving that he had himself together again. That he was ready to leave.

He'd be gone and she'd be left to pick up the pieces.

Chapter Ten

If only she'd found some way to stop him. Sarah shook her head as she drove toward the Caldwell mansion to pick up the children the next afternoon. That was wishful thinking, and she knew it.

Matt wouldn't be deterred from the expedition he'd made to the county courthouse in Beaufort in search of information about Sanders's real-estate deals. She hadn't bothered to try. He was one of the most single-minded people she'd ever met. In that respect he reminded her of her father.

Duty, honor, country had been her father's motto. Unfortunately his only daughter had come in a poor second to that.

She tried to rationalize away the sense of worry that had been hanging over her since the day before, when Matt had made it clear he wasn't finished with

Jason Sanders and his real-estate dealings. That concern wasn't caused only by her fear of making an influential enemy.

Matt was evading his own spiritual problems by concentrating on Sanders's possible misdeeds. She wasn't sure why she was so convinced of that, but she couldn't shake the feeling. Matt needed to heal. He needed to find peace, as Miz Becky had pointed out. He wouldn't do that by plunging headlong into a battle with someone he'd disliked since childhood.

She gripped the steering wheel.

Please, Lord. I'm not sure how to pray for Matt. I just know he has to turn to You, or he's never going to be at peace again. If I'm supposed to help him, please show me how to do it. I don't seem to be doing too well on my own.

She pulled between the twin pillars, shaded by century-old live oaks, that marked the circular drive of Twin Oaks, the Caldwell mansion. Matt's car pulled in just ahead of her. He'd gotten back from Beaufort then, with or without the information he'd gone after.

"Sarah." He got out and closed the door, waiting for her to catch up with him. "I thought you'd probably left the office by now, so I didn't bother to stop there."

"How did you make out at the courthouse?"

Matt lifted an eyebrow. "Are you sure you want to know?"

"I'll have to, won't I?" She looked up at him,

noting the lines of tension between his eyes. "If you're going to plunge the *Gazette* into controversy, I'd better know about it."

He leaned against the car, apparently preferring to have this conversation in the driveway, where no one could hear. "Controversy sells papers."

"Controversy also makes enemies." She'd learned that the hard way the first year they'd owned the paper. "A small-town paper can't afford to have too many of those if it's going to stay in business."

"That's a judgment call, isn't it?" He moved restlessly, his brow furrowed, and she could see that whatever peace he'd found a few days earlier had vanished now.

Guide me, Lord.

She could hear the children's voices from the back of the house, raised in play. All of her judgment of what to do had to be weighed in the balance of what was good for her children. That was what Matt didn't seem to understand.

"Why don't you tell me what you found out, and I'll tell you what I think?"

"No smoking gun, I'm afraid. But Sanders has been buying up a lot of small pieces of land down at the south end of the island, apparently for various private individuals."

"That doesn't sound so dire."

He frowned, drumming his fingers on the roof of the car. The sound played on her nerves. "Could be private home buyers, I suppose, but it seems odd that all his dealings lately have been in the same area.''

"Odd, but not illegal." She suspected that logic wouldn't stop him.

"Worth looking into a little more deeply, I think." He straightened, the movement taking him closer to her, and his tension seemed to leap the distance to dance along her skin.

"Sarah, I promise you I won't run anything unless I have proof, not just suspicion, of wrongdoing. Is that good enough for you?"

"I suppose it will have to be."

He frowned at her for a moment, looking as if he wanted to say something more, but a clamor of voices from the back lawn made him swivel in that direction. "Maybe we'd better see what all the noise is about."

She walked up the path beside him, hurrying a little. If her children were in trouble—

They rounded the corner of the house, and Sarah's heart sank. The picture in front of them was regrettably self-explanatory.

The gardener, Wanda's father, stood on one side of a trampled flower bed, ball cap pushed back on his gray hair, hands on his hips. Opposite him stood her two sons. Jeffrey's small face was a picture of guilt, while Ethan tried on a smile that was an echo of his father's. It didn't seem to be working on the gardener.

"Jeb, what's going on?" The sound of Matt's voice had the gardener turning to him.

"These two young rascals rampaged right through the marigold seedlings I just planted, that's what."

"It wasn't us," Ethan said quickly. "Honest, Mommy. It wasn't us."

Ethan turned the smile on her, and an image formed in her mind. Peter had worn that same winsome smile when he was about to spin a story about why he hadn't paid a bill or was overdrawn at the bank.

No. She rejected the image, overwhelmed with guilt. Peter was beyond his faults. She shouldn't think such things about him.

"Ethan…" she began.

"It was me." Andi scurried off the porch and ran to the gardener, tugging on his sleeve. "I'm sorry, Mr. Johnson. Really I am. I'll fix it."

The old man's face softened as he looked down at her. "I don't think so, missy."

"Those are Ethan and Jeffrey's footprints in the bed, Andi." Matt spoke before she could say anything else. His voice was a gentle, reassuring rumble. He knelt by the soft earth and pointed to the telltale sneaker prints.

This just kept getting worse.

"I'm sorry." Sarah hurried into speech. "I'm afraid this was a bad idea. I shouldn't have agreed to it." She looked at the gardener, because she didn't want to look at Matt. "I hope you'll let me repair the damage before we leave." And they wouldn't be coming back.

"Sarah, that's not necessary." Matt stood and took a step toward her.

"I told you I didn't want to cause problems for your family. I think it best if we go back to the way things were."

"The boys—" he began.

"The boys are my responsibility."

Hers, and hers alone. No matter how tempting it was to share her burden, she never should have let Matt take on even a little piece of it.

Matt frowned, trying to understand the distress on Sarah's face. She looked so distraught that his heart twisted. He had to talk to her about this, had to try and understand what she was feeling. But maybe he'd better defuse the situation with Jeb and the kids first.

He knelt next to the boys so that he looked from one small face to the other. "Seems to me you forgot what Wanda told you about the flowers."

They looked back at him, their blue eyes almost identical. For a moment he feared they wouldn't respond. Then Jeffrey's face crumpled. "I'm sorry." His voice was so soft, Matt could hardly hear it, but it gave him a sense of triumph. That was the first time he could remember that Jeffrey hadn't relied on Ethan to talk for him.

"We forgot," Ethan said quickly. He clutched Jeffrey's hand. "We didn't mean to do it. We're sorry."

"Since you're sorry, you'll want to help Mr. Johnson replant the flowers, won't you?"

Ethan swallowed visibly, giving Jeb a quick sidelong glance, then nodded. "If he'll let us."

Matt looked up at Jeb, knowing he could rely on the old man who'd been a fixture at Twin Oaks for as long as he could remember. "What do you say?"

Jeb shrugged, his face solemn but a twinkle lurking in his eyes. "Guess I can use a little help, all right." He fixed a firm gaze on the boys. "You younguns come over here, and I'll show you what to do."

Matt rose, taking Sarah's arm. "There," he said softly. "All settled."

"I don't think—"

"Leave it, Sarah." He nudged her away from the flower bed and toward the porch. "They'll learn more planting flowers with Jeb than they will from a lecture." He smiled. "Believe me, I speak from personal experience. Come and sit down, and leave it alone."

He could feel the reluctance in her, but she let him lead her to the steps. The back porch had its own swing, an old wooden one that had hung in the same spot as long as he could remember. They sat down, and the chains creaked as he pushed the swing with one foot.

"Now," he said gently, "let's talk about this nonsense. You're not going to back out on our arrangement because of one little hitch, are you?"

"I think it would be best." She sounded stubborn,

but there was something beyond stubbornness in her eyes, something that told him he'd have to push her for the truth.

"You remember the other day?" His hand brushed hers between them on the swing. "You told me I was overreacting when Amy got hurt."

That brought the ghost of a smile to her strained face. "You were."

"Well, now you are." He felt her start to protest and gripped her hand. It felt small and capable in his grip. "You are, Sarah. The boys were careless, that's all. They'll learn something. End of story."

She shook her head. "The children are my responsibility."

"Sure they are. I'm not trying to take that away. I just don't want you to throw away a good thing because of one little problem. That would be overreacting, Sarah. Wouldn't it?"

"Maybe." She sounded defensive, but at least she wasn't gathering up her kids and running for home. "I'm a single mother. That's natural enough."

So it was. All of Sarah's energy and devotion went to her kids, and that was the way it should be.

"You've been here nearly five years. That's long enough to have friends who are willing to help."

"Five years," she repeated. "Longer than I've been anywhere. Peter was always on the move, looking for the next opportunity. But I'm still the only one responsible for my kids. No one else."

He pushed the swing a time or two, wondering. "The other night I told you a lot more than I intended," he said, watching the boys chatter to Jeb, their guilt apparently forgotten, as he showed them how to set out the young plants. "Seems as if you could open up to me in return." He turned back to her, a challenge in his eyes.

She blinked. "I didn't mean to be rude. I just—" She stopped, took a breath. "No, I don't have any family. Peter and I were both only children. There's no one but me to take care of the children and provide for them. And since Peter didn't leave any insurance—"

"Wait a minute. Peter didn't leave any insurance?" He made it a question, hardly willing to believe he'd heard correctly.

She pulled her hand away from his, folding her arms defensively. "Well, naturally he never thought anything would happen to him."

"That's a poor excuse for leaving his family unprotected." Anger surged through him, and it showed in his voice.

It must have startled Sarah, too, because her gaze lifted, wounded and surprised, to his face. "I'm not sure that's any of your business."

The business—he latched on to that, confused at the rush of emotions her revelation had brought on. "He at least had mortgage insurance on the property.

I remember seeing that when we signed the agreement.''

She shook her head. "He canceled that. He said the premiums were too high."

"Too—"

Maybe he'd better not say anything else, because if he did he'd probably say something Sarah wouldn't forgive. Fortunately he heard Amy's waking-up cry.

Sarah got up quickly, obviously eager to end this conversation. "I'd better see to the baby." She whisked inside.

He shoved himself off the swing and took a couple of quick steps to the edge of the porch. The emotions that roiled inside him demanded action. A good long ride on the beach might help, but he could hardly go off at this point. Sarah would jump to the conclusion he was angry with her or the children.

"Look, Matt," Ethan called to him from the flower bed, waving a muddy trowel. "We planted almost a whole row. Jeb says they'll have flowers soon."

"Good job." He managed a smile. But watching the two boys working so diligently in reparation, Andi giggling with Jenny on the low branch of the live oak, little Amy, just waking in the room behind him, Matt couldn't believe their father had left them with no support, no safety net, nothing. How could any man do that?

He recognized the emotions that raced through him like blood through his veins. Anger. Jealousy. He was

furious with Peter Reed for leaving his family unprotected. And he was jealous. How could Sarah have
loved someone who'd been so unworthy of her? If
she loved him—

He stopped that thought, shocked at it. Sarah didn't
love him. He didn't want her to love him. He
couldn't. He'd decided, in the midst of tragedy and
horror, that he wouldn't take on the responsibility of
a family. Nothing had happened to change that.

Besides, in a few months he'd be gone. His life lay
out there, beyond the horizon. Sarah's lay here, where
she was so determined to put down roots for her family. That was the way it should be.

He wouldn't let himself feel anything for Sarah. He
couldn't.

Sarah pressed her cheek against the baby's soft
hair, trying to suppress the dismay that filled her. How
could she have done that? How could she have confided in Matt that way? It wasn't any of his business
what Peter had or hadn't done.

Her cheeks went hot with shame. She owed Peter
her loyalty, and telling Matt something negative about
him was a betrayal. She'd always been so careful to
tell the children nothing but good things about their
father. She didn't want them ever to know, ever to
think—

Maybe it was best not to finish that thought. She
went into the kitchen, carrying Amy. With any luck,

the boys had finished their planting by now. She'd gather her children and go home before anything else happened.

And would they come back the next day? She hesitated, wondering if Matt still sat in the swing. She didn't want to discuss the question with him again. She'd have to think about it, preferably well away from his disturbing presence.

She reached the screen door and stopped. Matt wasn't on the swing any longer. He sat on the top step of the porch, and Andi sat next to him. She was looking up at him with a solemn expression on her face.

"...they're my little brothers. Shouldn't I take care of them?"

Sarah held her breath. Should she go out and interrupt this conversation? Or should she stay out of it? Andi was her daughter, one part of her mind argued. She should be the one Andi came to with questions.

But she hadn't. Andi had come to Matt with this one. It would be wrong to try and prevent him from answering it.

"Well, you love them, right?" Matt didn't have any hesitation about dealing with this.

Andi sat up very straight. "I love them. Even when they tease me or get into my stuff."

Matt brushed the fringe of bangs back from Andi's

eyes, his big hand very gentle. "It must be hard to love them when they do things like that."

"I'm the oldest," Andi said, as if that were an irrefutable answer. "It's my job."

The lump in Sarah's throat would have kept her from speaking if she wanted to. Andi shouldn't have to feel so responsible. She was just a little girl herself.

"Sure it is." Matt's voice sounded gruff, as if he'd been affected by her daughter's answer, as well. "If you love somebody, then you want what's best for them, don't you?"

Andi nodded. "That's why I said I did it. So they wouldn't get in trouble." She leaned close to Matt, reaching up to tug his sleeve and bring him a little closer. "Ethan's afraid of Mr. Johnson," she whispered. "'Cause he has such a loud voice. But you can't tell. It's a secret."

Matt nodded solemnly. "I won't tell. But maybe it wouldn't be the best thing for Ethan if you took the blame." He pointed. "See? Ethan looks pretty happy, working with Mr. Johnson. I think he got over being afraid of him."

Andi looked as if she were puzzling over the moral dilemma. "Mommy says it's better to tell the truth. Do you think it's always better, even if it gets somebody you love in trouble?"

"Sugar, I think Mommy's right about this one. You can't cover up for people you love. It just makes things worse, for them and for you."

His words hit Sarah's heart like arrows. That was what she'd been doing with Peter. That was why she felt disloyal for letting it slip about the insurance. She'd been covering up for Peter, just as Andi tried to cover up for Ethan.

Oh, Lord, is that why she does it? Did Andi learn this from me?

The thought was a weight on her heart.

If I needed to learn this, maybe that's why You brought Matt into my life. So I'd see what was happening before it was too late.

"Mommy?"

Andi had glanced back, had seen her. Sarah struggled to compose her face as she stepped onto the porch. "Are you about ready to go, sweetie?"

Andi shook her head. "Matt says—"

"I heard." She tried to smile. "It sounds as if Matt was giving you good advice."

"Oh." Andi got up. "Well, I'll try to tell the truth all the time. But I'll bet Ethan isn't going to like it."

That surprised a laugh from her. "I think he'll learn to deal with it. You go get your stuff together now, okay?"

Andi skipped down the steps. "I'm going to leave my paper dolls here 'cause Jenny and me want to play with them again tomorrow. Wanda said she'll show us how to make new clothes for them. Okay?"

Was she doing the right thing? She could only hope so. "Yes, that's okay."

Her daughter ran off. Matt stood, the movement bringing him closer to her. "Does that mean you'll let the kids come again?"

"Yes." She had to force herself to look up at him, and when she did she seemed to get lost in his eyes. "Thank you, Matt." Her voice was barely more than a whisper.

"For what?" He took a step closer, and her breath caught. Being this close to him wasn't safe, not even in the middle of the afternoon with the children playing on the lawn.

"For what you said to Andi." She struggled to find the words. "You helped her in a way I hadn't been able to. Maybe you helped me, too. I'm grateful."

He took her hand in his, putting his other hand on the baby. His clasp was warm and strong. Protective. It had been a long time since she'd felt that anyone was protecting her.

"You're helping me," he said softly. "It seems like the least I can do."

"I hope I am," she said. She tried to mean it. She tried not to let herself think of what her life would be like when he was gone.

She'd told herself that she had her children, and that was enough. But every day she spent with Matt, he became dearer to her. Maybe just being a mother wasn't going to be enough for her anymore.

Chapter Eleven

Matt balanced the box of church history materials on one knee as he fumbled with the key to the newspaper office. The sun was just disappearing over the mainland, casting an orange glow that reflected from the windows of the closed office. Sarah would probably be tucking the children into bed about now, and he didn't want to disturb her.

The door opened, and he lugged the box Pastor Wells had given him inside and set it on the worn wooden counter. He was tempted to put it on Sarah's desk, but he had yet to convince her that this was one story she should handle.

He frowned down at the box. If he told her—

"Who's there?" Sarah's voice came sharply through the closed door to her apartment.

"It's Matt." He should have realized she'd hear him and might be alarmed. "Don't call the cops."

The door swung open, and Sarah stood there, barefoot, in jeans and a soft T-shirt. The light from the apartment turned her tumble of brown curls into a halo surrounding her face.

"You're lucky I didn't call them first." She stepped into the office and stopped, seeming to realize she didn't have shoes on. Then she shrugged and crossed to the counter opposite him. "I didn't know you planned to work late."

"I don't." He put a hand on the box. "I just wanted to drop this off. It's the materials Pastor Wells offered us."

"Great." She pulled at the box lid, blue eyes lit with excitement as if it contained buried treasure. He resisted the impulse to touch her cheek and helped her open the box instead.

Her enthusiasm didn't move him, he assured himself. He was just pleased, because that made it more likely she'd relieve him of the project.

"Since you're so interested in the church story, I hoped—"

Sarah looked up at him, and for a moment he lost his train of thought. He gave himself a mental shake. When had just looking at her started giving him this need to touch her? It was irrational.

"You hoped?" she prompted.

Back to business, Matt. "I thought you might like to take on this story."

She smiled, and he saw the dimple that was just like her daughter's. "And why did you think that? I was under the impression we were doing it together."

"Well..." His father had told him once that anyone who started a proposal with that word was in a poor negotiating position. His father was probably right. "I'm putting in a lot of hours on the real-estate investigation."

"Which might or might not turn into a story."

"You have a blunt way of putting things, you know that?" He leaned on the box, bringing his face closer to hers. "Can't we just say the church story isn't my cup of tea?"

"We could if we had a staff to pick up slack when one of us didn't want to do something." She pretended to look around the office. "Let me see... Where are they? Oh, that's right. It's just the two of us."

If she didn't look so appealing in her jeans and bare feet, he might be able to come up with something stronger in the way of argument. "All right, Madame Editor. What will it take to get you to do this story?"

Her face sobered. "You tell me the real reason you don't want to be involved, and I might consider it."

"That is the real reason."

She just lifted an eyebrow.

"All right." He heard the edge in his voice and

tried to suppress it. He seemed to have become transparent where Sarah was concerned. "It would bring me too close to too many memories. I don't think the paper will benefit from having a cynic who's angry with God doing a story like this. Is that what you want to hear?"

"Matt…" Her face got that troubled look it wore when one of her kids had done something wrong. He understood what it meant. She was worried about him.

His throat tightened. "It's okay," he muttered. "Just don't push me on this one, all right?"

"All right." The frown lingered between her brows. "I'll do the story, on one condition."

"What's that?"

"You go with me to the interviews." She held up a hand to stop his protest. "You know as well as I do that we have to talk with some of the older church members if the articles are to have any life at all. They know you. They'll talk if you're there." She grimaced. "Nearly five years here, but I'm still a newcomer in their eyes. How long does it take to belong?"

"Couple generations," he said lightly, then wished he hadn't. Sarah, with her longing to establish her family here, didn't need to hear that. "Just kidding," he said quickly. "Okay, you have a deal. I'll go along on the interviews, but you're writing the articles. Agreed?" He held out his hand.

"Agreed." She put her hand in his, smiling. But as his hand closed around hers, the smile faltered. Her eyes darkened.

Longing swept over him. He took a long breath, then lifted her hand to his lips. He kissed her wrist, feeling the rhythm of her pulse, knowing his own was beating just as fast.

"Sarah." He spoke her name, lips moving against her skin. It was a good thing the wooden counter stood between them, or he'd take her in his arms. For an instant he let himself visualize that, almost able to feel her softness against him. Then he shook his head. "You know this is driving me crazy."

"It—it's not doing me too much good, either." Her laugh trembled, and her lips looked very soft. "Maybe we should avoid tête-à-têtes in the future."

He dropped another kiss on the tender spot at the inside of her wrist, then let her go reluctantly. "A little hard, when we work together every day."

She took a step back. "That's business," she said. "We just have to remember that. It doesn't make sense for us to be anything more than partners. You'll be leaving, and—" She stopped, something shadowing her face. Regret, maybe?

"Yes. I'll be leaving." Surely he wasn't feeling regret, too, was he? Getting back to his real life was all he wanted. "But that doesn't mean we can't be friends, at least, as well as partners."

The office had grown dim with the setting of the

sun. He reached out to switch on the desk lamp, wanting to see her face.

But she turned away, straightening, as if facing up to something. "Friends. Of course we're friends." She looked back at him, her smile a little stiff. "I'll say good-night. I need to check on the children."

He stopped her with a touch on her arm, suddenly unwilling to let her go. "One thing. My father reminded me that the kick-off reception for the new resort hotel that's being built is Friday night at the yacht club. He wants his sons there, since he sold the land for the hotel."

She nodded. Of course she'd know about the Dalton Resorts Hotel that would be going up soon near the yacht club. "I suppose we should cover the reception. The new hotel is the biggest event on the island in a long time. Since you're going, you can do that."

"We should both be there. As you said, it's the biggest thing to come along in years. I want you to go with me, as my guest."

She gave him a level look. "I'm not sure that's such a good idea. Didn't we just decide—"

"This is business." He didn't know why it was so important to him; he just knew he wanted Sarah by his side that night. "And I agreed to do the church interviews with you, remember?"

He could sense the mixed feelings in her—the caution she wore as an armor against him battled with her anticipation. How long had it been since Sarah had had an evening out without her kids? Longer ago than she could remember, probably.

"Business," she repeated. "I guess as long as it's business, it's okay."

"Strictly business." He clasped her hand once, quickly, then turned to go. "Good night, Sarah. I'll see you tomorrow."

He'd better get out now, before she changed her mind about going with him. Irrational as it was, he wanted one lovely evening with Sarah before their time together was over. One lovely evening to remember.

"Now you sit right down there and make yourself comfortable." Matt's grandmother led Sarah to a padded rocker, then perched, upright and bright-eyed as a sparrow, on a straight chair. "Matt says y'all want to talk to me about the church."

Sarah glanced toward Matt. He'd done his best to efface himself, it seemed to her, choosing the chair that was farthest in the corner and leaning back as if this interview were no business of his.

"Matt and I are interviewing longtime church members for a series of stories on the church's bicentennial," she said, stressing his name a little. His gaze flickered toward her with a slightly amused look, as if he caught the point but didn't intend to cooperate.

Well, whether Matt cooperated or not, he was here.

If listening to the faith stories of people he cared about didn't reawaken his own spiritual side, she didn't know what would.

Is this the right thing, Lord? I want to help him turn to You, and this was the only thing I could think of that might help.

"Stories about the church?" Mrs. Caldwell's eyes lit with pleasure. "I 'spect you won't find anyone who knows more about it than I do. I've been going St. Andrews to worship for eighty years and counting. Now let me see…"

Sarah switched on the tape recorder and settled back to become lost in Naomi Caldwell's stories of when Caldwell Cove was young, life was harsh and all the islanders had to count on was faith and family.

Several stories later she glanced at Matt again. His gaze rested on his grandmother with a love that touched Sarah's heart. His face was relaxed, the tension and wariness gone from it.

"And then there's the dolphin," his grandmother said. "You've heard the story, a'course."

Sarah nodded. "Matt told me the legend—about the first Caldwell on the island and how he carved the dolphin for his bride as a symbol of their love. I'm sure we'll want to include that."

Some of the light went out of Naomi Caldwell's expression. "You'll have to tell about how it disappeared, too."

"There's no ending to that story." Matt spoke for

the first time since he'd greeted his grandmother. "It's an unsolved mystery, forty years old."

"If we look into it for the article, something new might come to light," Sarah suggested.

"I'm not sure that's a good idea." Matt's voice had gone flat, and the guarded expression was back on his face.

"Might be, at that." His grandmother looked at Matt, and Sarah almost imagined a challenge in her gaze. "Caldwells are s'posed to be married under that dolphin. That's what's meant."

"That's just an old wives' tale, Gran," Matt said quickly. "You know that. Cousin Chloe and her Luke seem happy enough, even without the dolphin there for their wedding."

"Things won't be put right 'til the dolphin's back where he belongs," his grandmother said stubbornly. "Maybe God means for the dolphin to be found again now, if y'all start looking."

Matt's jaw clenched. He didn't argue, but it was clear he didn't agree.

Just what was going on here? Matt and his grandmother seemed somehow at odds over the dolphin. It was almost as if they knew or suspected something about its disappearance.

Whatever the problem was, it had brought the familiar tension back to Matt's face. Sarah tried not to feel disappointed.

Reaching Matt wouldn't be done in a day. She just

had to remind herself that God was at work in him, whether Matt knew it or not.

This evening is business, Sarah told herself firmly. Business, nothing else. Unfortunately it was a little hard to convince herself of that with Matt's hand warm against her back as he guided her toward the yacht club entrance Friday night.

"I've lived here nearly five years, and this is my first time at the yacht club." She was probably babbling, but that was better than concentrating on the protective strength of his arm against her. "It's lovely."

White lights glittered from the long building, draping in graceful swags along the docks and reflecting in the dark water of the sound. She just hoped she didn't sound like an impressionable teenager on her first date.

"I don't exactly spend much time here myself." Matt took her hand as they went up the three steps to the porch that wrapped around the building. "My father does a lot of business here, though." He pulled open the door. "Well, thanks to him, it's our night to shine."

Piano music drifted on the air, mingling with the clink of glasses and the murmur of voices. The room was filled with the fragrance of expensive perfume, imported wine and old money.

Sarah smoothed her hand anxiously down the coral

silk of the only dress in her closet that had been re-
motely suitable for a dressy event. It had looked fine
in her bedroom, but it didn't look so appropriate next
to the designer models that studded the floor.

She looked at Matt, and her breath caught again at
the sight of him. He looked entirely too handsome in
that expensively tailored dark suit, his white shirt contrasting with his rich tan. He looked as if he belonged
here. She didn't, she reminded herself.

He smiled at her, chocolate eyes crinkling as if he
read her mind. "Don't look so scared. They're just
people."

"Not the kind of people I'm used to being
around." She touched her dress. "And I'm more
comfortable in jeans and sneakers."

He put his hand back on her waist, and she felt his
warmth through the thin silk. "You look beautiful,"
he whispered against her ear. "Every man in this
room is thinking that."

His breath stirred her hair, and she made a firm
effort to slow the racing of her heart. Business, she
reminded herself. She couldn't let herself give in to
the feeling that Matt's attentiveness meant anything.
This was business.

"Maybe we'd better circulate." She drew another
inch away from him. "We have to report on this
event, remember?"

He lifted the camera he had slung over his shoulder. "How could I forget, when you made me bring

this thing along?'' He nodded toward the small dance floor and lifted his eyebrow in the way that made her stomach flutter. ''Sure you wouldn't rather dance?''

''Business first,'' she said as firmly as she could, given the fact that butterflies seemed to have taken up residence under her rib cage.

''So after we get our story, you'll dance with me?'' He smiled at his advantage, as pleased as one of the kids at a promised treat.

She took an answer from her parenting mode. ''We'll see.''

''Matt.'' His father appeared before Matt could argue the point. ''Ms. Reed. Glad you could come.'' His gaze darted around the room while he spoke, as if he counted heads. ''Everyone's here. Be sure you get a photo of the bigwigs from Dalton Resorts, now.''

''I'll do that.''

Did his father recognize the stiffness in Matt's reply? Apparently not, because he gave them an automatic smile and moved on to another group. She wished she understood—

''Hey, Matt, you're here. Hi, Sarah. Quite a splashy do, isn't it?'' The woman who hugged Matt had a glow about her that said here was someone who'd found everything she wanted in life. Chloe Caldwell Hunter, Miranda's sister, had recently married and settled on the island. Sarah didn't know her as well as she knew Miranda, but she liked her.

"Mr. Dalton wants to make a good first impression." Luke Hunter smiled, holding out his hand to Matt, then put his arm around his new bride. "Looks like he and your father outdid themselves. Half the island is here."

"I haven't seen Miranda or your parents." Sarah glanced around, hoping to spot Miranda's bronze hair somewhere in the crowd. "I'd like—" She stopped, suddenly aware of an awkward silence.

"No." Color brightened Chloe's cheeks. "They won't be here. I'm sure the only reason we were invited was that Luke used to work for Dalton."

Sarah bit her lip. She'd obviously put her foot in something. A sudden flare of anger in Matt's eyes matched Chloe's embarrassment. What had she said?

"I'm sorry, Chloe." Matt bit off the words.

Chloe shrugged. "Not your fault, sugar."

"Come on, woman." Luke swung his wife toward the dance floor. "Let's enjoy the music."

"I'm sorry." Sarah spoke as soon as they were out of earshot. She could feel the heat in her cheeks. "I said something wrong, but I don't know what." She hadn't been here ten minutes, and already she'd managed to make a mess of things.

"It's not your fault." Matt clipped off the words. "Let's go out on the terrace and get some air."

She followed the pressure of his hand across the polished floor and out the French doors to the terrace. The door swung shut behind them, cutting off the buzz of conversation and music. Matt crossed to the rail, as if he wanted to get a little farther from it.

"I'm sorry," she said again. She went to lean against the railing next to him, looking out over the salt marsh. Spartina grass waved in the soft breeze, like ripples on a golden ocean, and the moon was a crescent sliver.

"I forgot you wouldn't know." Matt's voice had lost its edge. "It's one of those things that everyone on the island knows but nobody talks about."

"Except an outsider like me." This was the sort of inadvertent error that made her think she'd never belong here.

Matt's arm pressed against hers where their elbows were propped on the railing, and she felt the strength of his shoulder against hers—a strong shoulder, one a woman could put her head on and feel protected. His hand closed over hers.

"You're not an outsider. You just didn't know about it. No big deal."

The grip of his hand encouraged her to ask. "Why wasn't Chloe's family invited?"

His face was very close, close enough that she could see the muscle twitching at his jaw. "That would be my father's doing. He didn't want Clayton here. If he had a choice, he wouldn't speak to his brother at all."

"But—" Her mind raced, trying to understand.

"They were both at your grandmother's picnic. And you seem close to your cousins."

"My father and his brother both try to put a good front on it where Gran is concerned. Guess we have to be thankful their feud hasn't extended to the rest of the family."

"But why? What happened?"

He shrugged. "Nobody knows the whole story but them. Something happened when they were teenagers to drive a wedge between them. Besides which, they're as different as they can be. Uncle Clayton's content to be what Caldwells have always been and live the way Caldwells always have."

He stopped then, and she wanted to nudge him. "And your father?"

"My father—well, you've seen what he's like. Success means everything to him."

He almost spit out the last few words. Obviously he had an emotional stake in the whole thing.

"Brothers can be different without being enemies," she ventured.

"Not those two." His mouth twisted. "My father tends to use words like *shiftless* and *lazy* when it comes to his brother. And Uncle Clayton—" He stopped.

"What does your uncle say?" She murmured the words, wondering if he'd answer.

His grasp on her hand tightened painfully. "He says my father traded his honor for success."

"Is that what you think?" She couldn't believe she'd asked the question. He wouldn't answer. He'd tell her, politely of course, to mind her own business.

"He's my father." He ground out the words.

She put her other hand over his where it clasped hers, willing him not to close her out. "He's your father. But you're an adult. Sometimes it's hard to start looking at our parents with adult eyes."

"That sounds like the voice of experience speaking." He turned the comment back on her.

"I guess I had trouble with that one," she admitted. "For a long time I was angry with my father for putting the army first after my mother died. I felt as if I always came in second. I resented being dragged all over the world. If he loved me, why wouldn't he settle down and give me a home?"

"You still feel that way?"

She took a deep breath, inhaling the pungent aroma of the marsh. "After I had children of my own, I looked at it a little differently. I think Dad just didn't know what to do with me after Mom died. He tried. It can't have been easy for him, either, but he thought it was right to keep me with him." She shook her head, knowing her voice sounded choked. "I just wish I'd come to that understanding before he died. He knew I loved him, but I'd like to have cleared the air with him."

He turned so that they faced each other, very close, their hands still clasped between them. "That's why belonging here in Caldwell Cove is so important to you, isn't it?''

''Building a stable home for my kids is the most important thing in the world to me. We need to belong here.'' She tried to smile. ''But maybe you were right. It takes a couple of generations.''

''No.'' He said it so quickly she knew he heard the fear in her voice. ''I didn't mean that. Of course you belong here. So what if you don't know every little thing that's happened?''

''Seems to me your family feud is a pretty big thing.'' She looked up at him. She couldn't see him distinctly in the darkness, but that didn't really matter. His features were clear in her heart.

''Trivia,'' he said firmly. ''You know the important stuff, and you're learning more every day. Don't you think people notice the love and care you put into every story, whether it's the charity drive or the middle school science fair? It shows, Sarah.''

''I'd like to believe that.'' She could hear the longing in her voice.

''You can believe it.'' As if he didn't know how else to reassure her, he drew her into his arms. ''You belong here,'' he whispered against her hair.

His cheek was warm against hers. She put her hands on his chest, feeling the steady beat of his heart. *You belong here,* he'd said. He'd meant she belonged in Caldwell Cove.

Unfortunately where she wanted to belong was in his arms...forever.

Chapter Twelve

What was she going to do with this information? Sarah sat at her desk several days later, staring with dismay and consternation at the notebook she'd unearthed from Pastor Wells's box of church history. How could she possibly tell Matt that his father had been suspected of the theft of the carved dolphin from the Caldwell Cove church?

She leafed through the pages of cramped handwriting by the then-pastor of St. Andrews. This appeared to be a kind of personal journal he'd made during his years on the island. Pastor Wells couldn't have known about it; he'd never have given so inflammatory a document to Matt knowingly.

The notebook had been stuffed inside a church register. It seemed far more likely Pastor Wells had just dumped everything he thought might be interesting into the box, never realizing the notebook existed.

Her eyes were drawn unwillingly back to the pertinent page. After expressing the grief and shock that accompanied the discovery that the carved dolphin was missing from the sanctuary, he added his conclusions.

Although I can prove nothing, I keep remembering the day I found the two Caldwell boys in the sanctuary with one of the summer visitors— Emily Brandeis. Someone had taken the dolphin down, and the girl held it. Jefferson was quick to say that she just wanted to see the dolphin, but now—

His notes cut off there, as if he'd been reluctant to put anything else into words. But what he'd said was enough to make his suspicions clear.

Her hands clenched the notebook. She could bury it back in the bottom of the box. Matt would never look. He'd made it clear he didn't want to be involved with the church story.

She seemed to see him, standing on the terrace in the moonlight, talking about his mixed feelings for his father. If she showed him this, it would simply cause more trouble between them. But did she have the right to hide it?

Please, show me what to do. I don't know what's right. Please.

"Sarah? Is something wrong?"

She jerked, pressing her hands down on the telltale notebook pages, and looked up at Matt. "You startled me. I didn't hear you come in."

"Maybe we should put the bell back," he said. He crossed to her, lifting an eyebrow in inquiry. "What were you so intent on that you didn't hear the door open?"

"It's nothing." The evasion came out before she considered, and she was appalled at her instinctive wish to conceal it from him. Memories flashed through her mind—Matt telling her not to manipulate him, even for his own good; the things they'd told each other that night on the terrace; the way she'd felt when he'd held her protectively in his arms.

He leaned against the desk, regarding her with a serious expression. "You don't look as if it's nothing. Level with me, Sarah."

She'd asked God to show her what to do with this knowledge. Was He giving her an answer? She stared for a moment at the rain-swept street outside, then made up her mind.

Slowly she held out the notebook to him. "I found this stuffed in with the materials Pastor Wells sent over. I'm sure he didn't know it was there. I think you'd better look at it."

Watching his face as he read the journal was like

watching flesh turn to stone. He went through it twice, then flipped slowly through the succeeding pages, obviously looking for more.

She'd already done that. She knew there was nothing else, except for the pastor's mournful conclusion that they'd probably never know the truth.

"I'm sorry," she said at last, when it seemed he'd never speak again. "I didn't want to show you, but—" She faltered then, unable to go on.

"You had to show me." He closed the notebook carefully, but his strong hands twitched as if he'd like to rip it into pieces. He looked at her, his face shuttered. "I suppose you think I should talk to my father about this."

She folded her hands in silent prayer. *Please.* "I'm not much of an expert on father/child relationships, am I? But, yes, I think you have to talk to him. Otherwise you'll just go on suspecting him, when maybe there's some explanation."

"Somehow I doubt that." He tossed the notebook on her desk. "Maybe the smartest thing to do is to bury that thing wherever it's been for the last forty years."

She looked at him, sensing the pain under the mask he wore. Did he really believe he could do that?

"Your grandmother wants you to find the truth."

His hands clenched. "I think my grandmother already knows, or at least suspects."

That could be the undercurrent she'd thought she

noted when Matt and his grandmother talked about the dolphin. "What makes you think so?"

Every muscle in his body seemed to tense. And every cell in her body seemed aware of that. For a long moment she thought he'd launch himself off her desk, stride out of the office, running away from the thing he didn't want to face. Finally he shook his head, as if telling himself that wasn't an option.

"I heard them once—my grandmother and grandfather. I was just a kid, playing cowboys and Indians in the garden, trying to creep up on them without letting them know I was there." His mouth twisted. "Worked better than I expected. They didn't hear me, but I heard them. They were talking about my father."

Her heart was breaking for him. "I'm sorry."

He shook off her sympathy with a brief shake of his head. "You never knew my grandfather. Even as a kid, I recognized what he was—a man of integrity, all the way through. Maybe he never had more than two dimes to rub together, but every person on the island respected him, like they do my uncle Clayton."

What could she say, when she feared he was right? "Did they say something about the dolphin?"

"My grandfather thought my father had been involved. Said he'd tried to talk to him, straight out, and my father denied it. Grandpa didn't believe him."

She saw the truth then, so clearly, and wondered if

he'd ever admitted it to himself. "That's why you left, isn't it?"

He flinched as if she'd struck him, and she thought he'd deny it. After a long moment he shook his head. "I don't know, Sarah. I wanted to make a name for myself out there. But how much of that had to do with my feelings about my father—I just don't know."

"You never talked to him about it, did you?"

He gave her a wry smile. "You're a good journalist, Sarah. You know all the right questions. No, I never talked to him about it, not even when I was a teenager and butted heads with him at every turn. I could never say that his values disappointed me."

She sent up another frantic silent prayer. *Please don't let me make a mistake.*

"Maybe it's time you resolved that."

Anger flashed briefly in his eyes. "Like you resolved things with your father?"

She looked back at him steadily. "I don't want you to wait until it's too late, like I did."

He stood, staring down at her, the anger fading slowly from his face. She sensed the instant in which he made a decision. He picked up the notebook.

"Maybe talking to him about this will be a step in that direction."

Her throat was so tight she could only nod. He was right. Confronting his father about the dolphin was a step to resolving his feelings about him.

It was probably also another step toward Matt being ready to leave Caldwell Cove for good.

Hours later, Sarah's head jerked up at the sound of the door. Her nerves were strung as fine as fishing line, waiting for Matt's return. But it wasn't Matt; it was his grandmother. She came in, shaking rain from her umbrella.

"Mrs. Caldwell." She hoped she didn't sound disappointed. "How nice to see you. I'm afraid Matt's not here right now."

"Don't reckon that matters." She marched, erect as a woman half her age, to the counter. "I found some old pictures of the church I thought maybe you could use, if you want them."

"That's wonderful." She took the rumpled, used envelope. A sheaf of faded, black-and-white photos spilled out onto the counter. "Pastor Wells gave us a box of things, but there weren't many photos in it." She cringed inwardly at the memory of what it had contained.

Mrs. Caldwell seemed to hear something she didn't say. "Where did you say Matt was?"

"He—he went back to the house. He wanted to talk to his father about something." She couldn't say any more, couldn't give Matt's secrets away, even to someone who loved him as much as his grandmother did.

"I see." Naomi Caldwell's wise old eyes probed,

as if she looked right through Sarah's face and into her soul. "'Bout time that boy had things out with his father. He keeps too much inside himself. And takes on too much responsibility, like he has to save the whole world. Always has been like that."

Sarah thought about the little boy who'd taken on the schoolyard bullies to defend the smaller children, about the man who couldn't compromise the truth, even when it hurt him.

"Maybe he has. That's not a bad thing. The world needs—" she hesitated, searching for the right word "—warriors."

Matt's grandmother nodded, as if something satisfied her. "Reckon you're right at that. Trouble is, sometimes he's so busy righting wrongs, he doesn't stop to see that God can even bring good out of terrible things."

"That's the verse you gave him, isn't it?

"And we know that in all things, God works for the good of those who love Him, who have been called according to His purpose."

"He told you that, did he?" His grandmother smiled. "Someday Matt will see the truth of that. I just hope—" She paused, looking at Sarah searchingly. "You know, that boy has a powerful lot of love dammed up inside him to give someone."

Sarah felt as if the wise old woman had just lifted a lid and looked into her heart. Oddly enough, it didn't hurt.

"It might take someone very special to help him release that love." *And I'm afraid it's not me, however much I might want that.*

"Reckon that's in God's hands, if Matt will let it be."

"Yes," she said softly. *It was in God's hands, not hers.*

Mrs. Caldwell patted the pictures. "Well, guess that's all I came in for." She turned to go, then paused. "You know, ever since Matt was a boy, if he was upset about somethin', he'd be out riding that horse of his on the beach. I guess, if someone wanted to find him, that's where he'd be."

There didn't seem to be much left in Sarah's heart that Naomi Caldwell's wise old eyes hadn't seen. And someone did want to find him.

For the first time Matt could remember, this wasn't working. He slowed Eagle to a trot, patting the horse's damp mane. The rain had stopped, to be replaced by a gray fog that closed in around him, making him feel as isolated as if he were the only man left on earth.

Cantering along the hard-packed sand still made him feel as if he were flying, but it didn't erase his father's words from his mind. The beach didn't take him far enough away to do that.

Sarah's insight echoed in his heart. *Had* he gone away because of the clash between his father's values and his own? He'd had plenty of good reasons to leave Caldwell Island, but he'd never admitted the one she'd seen.

Her clear view into his heart dismayed him. Made him want to run, just like talking to his father had made him want to run—to go back out into that other world and find other dragons to fight.

He glanced ahead, seeing a figure silhouetted dark against the mist, waiting where the path went up through the dunes toward the house. He didn't have to see any better to know who it was. Sarah waited for him.

He slowed Eagle to a walk, patting the horse's neck. Eagle snorted, as if asking to continue their run.

"No," he said aloud, as if the horse had asked. "I guess I can't avoid this."

Sarah put up her hand to hold back the tangle of brown locks that curled wildly from the damp air. She got up from the sea-whitened log she'd been sitting on. How had she known he'd be here? Maybe the bigger question was, how did she know so much about him?

In a few short weeks, Sarah had found her way into the inner recesses of his heart. Worse, she and her little family had made him start dreaming again of things he'd made up his mind he'd never have.

Couldn't he? a treacherous little voice asked inside his mind. Couldn't he have a life like a normal person?

The answer he pledged himself to sprang out quickly. He couldn't. He'd seen too much, done too much. He wasn't the innocent he'd been when he left Caldwell Cove, and he couldn't be that person again. Sarah and her kids didn't need an embittered cynic in their lives. They deserved better.

"Sarah." Eagle stopped automatically when they reached her, as if Matt's body language had already told him that this was a person they didn't pass by.

For a moment something in him resisted. He didn't want to talk to Sarah now—didn't want to talk to anyone. This was his problem, and he'd handle it his own way. But even before he'd finished the argument in his mind, he'd dismounted.

"I was worried about you." She reached up to pat Eagle's neck, but her eyes were on Matt. "You didn't come back."

"I needed to get it out of my system. Riding does that for me."

The worry in her face was diluted with a slight smile. "That's what your grandmother said. She came to the office."

"You didn't tell her—" Alarm ran along his nerves like a warning signal.

"No. I didn't tell her." She lifted her shoulders in a helpless shrug. "But I'm not sure I fooled her at all. She just seems to know things."

A few pointed memories flickered through his

mind, almost making him smile. "Yes, she does, doesn't she?"

Sarah straightened, and he saw her throat work as she swallowed. "How did it go?"

How could he tell her? How could he not? She was the one who'd found it, after all.

She shook her head quickly. "Look, I'm sorry. I'm not asking you to confide in me."

"Aren't you?"

"No," she said firmly, in much the same way she responded to Amy's attempts to touch something hot. "But you have to talk to someone, Matt. What about your brother?"

You already know more about me than anyone else, maybe including Adam.

"I've never talked to Adam about my father. If I were guessing, I'd say he knows how I feel. But Adam—well, Adam's made his own separate peace with who Dad is."

That was true—he realized as he said it. No one ever doubted his brother's integrity, but Adam apparently didn't feel the need to confront their father over it.

A bitter taste filled his mouth, and he turned away so she wouldn't see what he felt. He stroked Eagle's strong neck, feeling the moisture on the silky skin from the gallop that hadn't taken him far enough away. Somewhere out in the mist a foghorn sounded, deep and lonely.

Sarah covered his hand with hers, stilling its restless movement. Hers was small but strong, just like the woman herself. Sarah was strong enough to bear his bitterness. It scared him how much he wanted to tell her, wanted to feel her sympathy, like salve on a wound.

"I talked to him." The words came out in a rush, as if they couldn't be spoken fast enough. "I showed him the notebook."

Her fingers curled around his. She was close enough that he could smell the faint flowery scent she wore, close enough that he could feel the intake of her breath. They stood inside a circle of fog that encompassed them, cutting them off from the rest of the world.

"He denied it, of course." His voice was flat. "Said the minister had it in for him, said none of it was true."

"You didn't believe him." Her voice was as soft as the mist that touched her hair with moisture.

"No." He hadn't believed his father. He'd seen the spurt of panic before the lie that came so easily. "I almost walked away, then." He wasn't proud of that.

"But you didn't."

"I pushed him. And finally he came out with the story."

She didn't say anything. Just waited. But he could feel her warmth surrounding him, diluting the bitterness that came with the memory of his father's words. He knew he was going to tell her.

"He and my uncle were teenagers that summer. There was a girl—a daughter of one of the summer visitors, the yacht club crowd. Usually they didn't mix with islanders, but he said Emily Brandeis was different. Emily wanted to be with them. And it sounds like both of them were in love with her."

"She wanted the dolphin." Sarah seemed to have the same ability to read between the lines that his grandmother did.

"He said she teased them about getting the dolphin figure for her, so she'd have a memento of their summer."

Eagle tossed his head, chasing the mist, his movement the only thing that stirred. Sarah was so still, she might have been carved from wood herself.

"He didn't say so, but I'd guess this Emily favored my uncle. So one night, when a group of young people were having a picnic out on Angel Isle, he slipped the dolphin out of the chapel. He says he just wanted to show it to her, I guess to impress her."

He stopped, reliving the anguish he'd felt at those words on his father's lips. Sarah's fingers tightened on his. He could feel the warmth flowing from her. It was like a balm, coming from her gentle spirit straight to his troubled soul.

"There was some trouble—he wasn't very specific about that part of it. The party was raided by a bunch of yacht club parents. In all the confusion, he lost sight of the dolphin.'' He shook his head. ''I'm not sure whether I believe that or not. He says he went back the next day, after things calmed down, but the dolphin wasn't there. And when he went to ask Emily, she and her family had left the island. My father claims he never saw it again.''

''Do you believe him?''

He shrugged. ''I'm not sure what I believe. And even if I were, what would I do with it? I certainly can't tell my grandmother that her son was responsible. It would be different if I could get the dolphin back for her, but I can't.''

Sarah reached up to touch his face then, turning it so he was looking at her. He didn't know what he expected to see in her face, but all he found there was caring and sympathy. ''Maybe it's not too late. If we pursued this Emily, we might find something.''

''That's assuming there's any truth to what my father said.''

''Perhaps you should assume that, unless it's proved otherwise.''

He managed a smile. ''I hate to point this out, but that's the exact opposite of what any good investigative reporter would do.''

''In this case, you're a son first, a reporter second.'' Her touch took any criticism out of her words. ''I think we need to try at least.''

He put his hand over hers, pressing her palm

against his cheek, feeling her generous heart speaking to him. "What makes you such a wise woman, Sarah Reed?"

Warm color surged under her skin. "I'm not so wise. But I do know you have to go on loving someone, even when he's disappointed you."

"Who are we talking about, Sarah?" he asked softly. "My father? Yours? Or Peter?"

He saw that hit home and knew she had been thinking, in some way, of her late husband.

"That doesn't matter," she said. "If someone you love does something wrong—well, love wouldn't be love if it stopped then." She gave him a ghost of a smile. "God doesn't stop loving me, even though I know how often I disappoint Him."

She was so serious, so intent on mending him. He didn't want to disappoint her.

He put a kiss on her palm, then closed her fingers around it and moved a careful inch away, so he wouldn't be tempted to do more. "All right," he said. "We'll assume the best and try to find out the truth. I just hope we're not disappointed."

A smile blossomed on her face, and he knew what he was really thinking. *I don't want to disappoint you, Sarah. I don't ever want to disappoint you.*

Chapter Thirteen

Sarah stared absently at her computer screen the next morning, trying to concentrate on the day's work and knowing she couldn't. She couldn't get Matt off her mind.

There couldn't be a future for them. They both knew that. Admitting their mutual attraction should make dealing with it easier, but somehow it hadn't.

Well, attracted or not, God had laid a burden on her heart. She had to help Matt heal, and one of the big pieces of that healing must be his relationship with his father. Until he'd managed that, he'd probably not be ready to resolve things with his Heavenly Father.

Finding out what had happened to Emily Brandeis and the church's dolphin carving might go a long way toward that, but that search was proving unexpectedly difficult. She frowned at the records she'd called up on the computer, trying to see them instead of the pain in Matt's eyes when he'd talked about his father.

She heard the door and glanced up to see Matt's tall figure silhouetted against the June sunshine. He stepped into the office, and she saw that he was smiling.

"You're looking pleased. Has something happened?"

He crossed the office to perch on the corner of her desk. "I found out something interesting."

Her mind leaped to her own search. "About Emily?"

For an instant he looked blank. "Emily? No. About Jason Sanders." He lifted an eyebrow. "Would it surprise you to learn that every person for whom Sanders negotiated a purchase down on the south end was a friend or relative of his?"

"Well." She paused to assimilate that. "That's not illegal."

"No, but it is odd." Matt's smile had an edge to it. This must be how he looked when he tracked down an important story. A chill touched her. He looked different from the Matt she'd grown to know.

"What are you going to do about it?"

"I have some feelers out for information. Someone knows what's going on. Something will come in," he said confidently. "If Sanders is up to something dis-

honest, everyone's going to read about it on the front
page of the *Gazette*.''

She knew what else he was thinking—that breaking
a big story would go a long way toward showing his
bosses he was ready to go back to work. She tried to
ignore the ball of lead in her stomach at the thought.

''Now, what's this about Emily?'' Matt seemed to
shift gears.

''Nothing, unfortunately.'' She flung out her hand
toward the computer screen. ''I thought it would be
fairly easy to find out what happened to her when she
left the island, and for a time it was. Did you know
that her father wasn't quite the success people seemed
to believe?''

He leaned closer, his attention caught. ''All I know
is what my father said, and that's not much. I certainly got the impression Emily was one of the yacht
club crowd.''

''Brandeis's business apparently crashed not long
after their visit to the island that summer. But Emily
married well—a Savannah society type. Unfortunately it didn't last. There was a divorce, then a re-
marriage. She was on the fringes of Savannah society
for a while. Then—nothing.'' She smacked her hand
on the desk in frustration. ''She vanishes from public
record.''

He stood up abruptly, startling her. ''Let's go to
Savannah.''

''What?'' She looked up into smiling brown eyes

and felt a betraying weakness flow through her. "When?"

"Now." He held out his hand.

"We can't just take off for Savannah." She scrambled for a good reason why she couldn't go with him. Alone. For the day.

"Why not?" He caught her hand, drawing her to her feet. Seeing his investigation into Sanders bearing fruit seemed to have given him confidence. "The kids are fine at the house."

"If we go into Savannah, we probably won't be back at the time I usually pick them up. I can't leave them there."

"Why not?" he said again. "Wanda would be happy to watch them, and Jenny'd be delighted to have Andi stay for supper."

"It's an imposition." She let the pressure of his hand pull her a step closer, trying to find the will to resist the attraction.

His smile said he knew exactly what she was doing. "Come on, Sarah. I thought you wanted to help me solve this mystery for my grandmother."

I want to help solve it for you, she thought. "How do you know we'll find anything there? Emily could have left Savannah ages ago."

"Possibly," he conceded. "But I'm betting she didn't. If there's one thing I know about old-time Savannahians, it's that they tend to stay put. I believe

Emily Brandeis wouldn't stray too far, if she had a choice.''

She felt herself weakening. ''I suppose it wouldn't hurt. I should call and talk with Wanda first.''

''We'll do better than that.'' His fingers tightened compellingly on hers. ''We'll stop by the house on our way off-island. Come on, Sarah. It'll do us good to chase down this shadow together.''

Together. How many more things would they be likely to do together? Matt would leave. She had no doubts about that. Couldn't she have one more memory to savor when he was halfway around the world?

''All right.'' She picked up her bag, knowing she was rationalizing this. ''We'll go.'' Because she wanted to be with him, even knowing there was no future in this. She just wanted to be with him while she could.

''Pretty depressing looking.'' Matt looked from the run-down boardinghouse in a seedy Savannah neighborhood to Sarah's face. It reflected just what he was thinking. Emily Brandeis's life had gone steadily downhill after that summer she spent on the island.

''This is a far cry from the mansion over on Bull Street, isn't it?'' Sarah said.

He nodded. ''One bad marriage after another, apparently. Funny. The way Dad described her, she was the kind of golden girl who had the world at her feet.''

''Maybe that's how she seemed, to him,'' Sarah said gently. ''He was young, and it sounds as if she was his first love.''

Something tightened inside him. ''She married for money and position.'' Just as his father had. If it hadn't been for his wife's money, Jefferson Caldwell's life, and hence his sons' lives, might have been very different. Or would he have found another way to the success and status he craved? Maybe things would have turned out the same in any event.

Luckily Sarah couldn't know what he was thinking. She glanced again at the boardinghouse, and distress was evident in her eyes. ''Aren't we going in? If she's there, she might be willing to talk.''

He shouldn't have brought her. She was more affected than he'd guessed she would be by this old story. He hadn't really believed, when he'd suggested this little expedition, that they'd find anything useful. He might as well admit it. He'd just wanted to spend the time with her.

''We've come this far.'' He took Sarah's arm. ''I guess we may as well go through with it.''

They started up curving stairs whose wrought iron railing had probably been beautiful before years of neglect.

''You were right about one thing.'' Sarah stepped over a paper bag blown by the wind against the rail.

''What's that?'' He lifted the knocker and let it fall.

''Savannahians don't go far from home.''

"No." Somehow being right didn't give him much pleasure at the moment. "She might not be in the Bull Street mansion any longer, but she's still in the city."

"Yeah, what?" The woman who flung the door open wore a St. Patrick's Day celebration T-shirt that stretched over her ample frame and argued with the garish orange of her hair. "You want something?"

"We're looking for Emily Watson." He used the last married name they'd found for her. "I understand she lives here."

"You relatives?" She looked them up and down. "You don't look like you belong in this part of town. Always said she come from money, but I never saw none of it."

"No, we're—" What were they? He suspected she wouldn't be forthcoming to reporters unless there was something in it for her.

"Friends of the family," Sarah said. "May we see her?"

The woman let out a short burst of laughter. "Reckon you'll have to go to Bonaventure Cemetery if you want to do that. She died three months ago."

The depth of his disappointment shocked him. He hadn't realized until that moment how much he wanted to resolve this situation—to find the missing dolphin, to heal the family feud, to bring his father back into the Caldwell clan.

"I'm so sorry to hear that, Mrs.—?" Sarah's voice

was soft, sympathetic. "You must have become friends while she lived here. I'm sure it was a loss."

He was almost equally surprised to see the woman assume the air of a mourner at Sarah's words.

"Mrs. Willie, Gina Willie. I guess you could say that. I was probably her only friend."

"She didn't have any family?" Sarah asked.

"Well, she had a daughter," the woman admitted grudgingly. "Lived up north someplace though. Didn't come here much, 'til her mama got sick."

"I suppose she took care of all the arrangements after her mother's death—disposing of her belongings and so forth?" Matt held his breath. Were they actually likely to find some trace of the dolphin at this late date?

"The daughter packed up what she wanted. Left some clothes for me to give away. Emily didn't have much."

"I don't suppose you ever saw a wooden figure of a dolphin, about so high." He measured with his hands.

"Somethin' valuable, was it?" The woman's eyes narrowed suspiciously.

"Just something that belonged to the family." His family. "Did her daughter take it?"

But she was already shaking her head. "Never saw nothing like that."

He thought of his grandmother, mourning the loss of the dolphin even as she kept the story alive for each generation. He wanted to make this better for her.

"Do you have the daughter's address?" he asked abruptly.

The woman took a step back, her suspicion flaring again. He could sense Sarah's tension, as if she wanted this just as much as he did.

"If you're family friends, guess you'd know that yourself." The woman snapped the door closed in their faces.

Frustrated, he lifted his fist, ready to hammer until she opened up again, but Sarah caught his arm.

"Better leave it, before she decides to call the police."

He glared at the closed door. "I don't like dead ends."

"At least we found out what happened to Emily. Now that we know the daughter exists, we can find her."

"I wanted to come home with answers."

"You did a good thing today, Matt." Her voice was warmly encouraging. "Don't beat yourself up because you couldn't solve a forty-year-old problem in a day."

He had to smile, because that was exactly what he was doing. He took her arm to pilot her back down the narrow stairs, enjoying the feel of her softness against him.

"How did you get to know me so well, Sarah?"

"Just a lucky guess." She seemed to try for lightness, but he heard the undertone of emotion in her voice. Worse, he knew that his own had grown husky when he asked the question.

What's going on with us, Sarah? This isn't supposed to happen.

But it was.

"Sure you didn't want dessert?" Matt looked down at her as they left the restaurant overlooking the harbor, and she suppressed the familiar flutter of her pulse at his nearness. "They make a Key lime pie that's out of this world."

Sarah shook her head firmly. "I'd burst if I ate another bite. The dinner was fantastic." Also very elegant. She'd protested that she wasn't dressed for a fancy restaurant, but Matt had insisted she looked fine and had whisked her inside anyway.

He'd probably wanted to remove the taste of sadness, for both of them. And it was sad. Lovely Emily, the golden girl, had ended up poor and alone, with all her bright promise gone.

Sarah glanced again at Matt's face as they crossed the cobblestone street along the waterfront. He steered her carefully around a clutch of tourists, intent on seeing every shop in the renovated cotton warehouses, and onto the brick plaza. The lampposts created circles of light in the gathering gloom.

He hadn't said much about their day's search—

he'd talked Savannah history all through dinner. But the frown lines between his brows told her he still thought about it.

They stopped, leaning against the wall and looking out over the water. A white paddle-wheeler moved slowly past them, white lights outlining its wrought iron railings, a calliope playing. Through lighted windows, she could see dinner being served.

"Nice way to spend an evening."

"The *Georgia Queen*," he said. "Going for an evening dinner cruise."

Behind them, the bell in the old city hall chimed, then struck the hour. Nine o'clock.

"It's getting late," she said. "I should go home."

"The kids are fine." His arm pressed against hers where they leaned on the wall. "You can't rush away without enjoying the view." He pointed to the island across the sheet of silver water. "That's Hutchinson Island. The building is the convention center. Down that way is Tybee Island, where the elite of Savannah used to go to escape the summer heat."

She stirred, remembering. "If Emily's family had gone there instead of to Caldwell Island that summer, things might have been different."

"Funny, I was just thinking that." He frowned absently at a brown pelican that rocked on the current. "Still, you never know. Sometimes I think things would have turned out the same, no matter what happened."

"Sounds awfully fatalistic." She wondered if he was thinking about his father and the dolphin, or about his friend, dying far from home.

"I guess it does." Now it was his turn to move restlessly. "If I said that to Gran, she would remind me that all things work together for good."

She hesitated. Matt had just opened a door to her, quite unexpectedly, and she wanted to choose her words carefully.

"You can't leave out the rest of the verse. '...In all things, God works for the good of those who love Him, who have been called according to His purpose.'"

She felt him stiffen. "What difference does that make?"

Please, Lord, give me the right words. "I've come to believe it means that if we're trying to do God's will, He can bring good things out of even our mistakes."

His gaze searched her face, and she thought she read longing in it, instead of the cynicism she'd come to expect. "Is that coming from your own experience?"

A boat whistle came from out of the dark, sounding lonely. She owed him a truthful answer, even though it might be difficult. He put his hand over hers, and his touch gave her the strength to continue.

"What we learned about Emily today—it sounded

as if she married for all the wrong reasons. I guess I related to that.''

His fingers tightened on hers. ''You didn't marry for money or position, Sarah.''

She had to smile. ''No, certainly not that. But I told you a little about what my life was like with my dad. The constant moving, never having a home of our own, really had an effect on me. I think, now, that when I fell in love with Peter, I was just longing for a home of my own.'' She shook her head. ''That's not a good enough reason to get married.''

''What was Peter looking for?'' His voice was a low rumble that was somehow comforting.

She thought about the charming, irresponsible young man who'd captured her needy heart. ''I think maybe Peter wanted someone to hold on to. Someone who'd be his anchor.''

''People have married for worse reasons.''

''I suppose so.'' She shook her head, realizing that for the first time she was looking honestly at her marriage, instead of trying to surround it with some sort of halo. ''I'm trying to say that I might have imposed my dream on Peter. That maybe it never was his.''

''The dream of a home and a family.'' There was something strained in the way he repeated the words.

''Yes. Maybe I pushed him to be someone he was never meant to be.''

He laced his fingers through hers. The pressure of his palm against hers was surprisingly intimate. ''Peter was a grown-up,'' he said. ''Whatever happened, he made his own mistakes.''

''If we made mistakes, if our marriage wasn't part of God's plan for our lives, He still brought good out of the consequences.'' She felt her way through, only realizing what she'd come to believe as she verbalized it. ''Even if I was wrong, God was faithful. I have the children. They're worth anything.''

''That's true for you. But I can't accept that the blowing up of that mission station led to anything good.'' His voice had turned harsh with pain.

Am I failing him, Lord? Give me the words.

''I know it's hard.'' She put her other hand over their clasped hands, trying to infuse him with her concern. ''But we don't know what all the results of that act are. Maybe we never will.'' She was losing him, she knew it. ''What would your friend say, if you could ask him?''

For a moment she thought he wouldn't answer. Then he let out a breath, and the corner of his mouth twitched. ''He'd say, 'Quit trying to play God, Caldwell. You're not big enough.'''

''He sounds like someone special.''

''He was that.'' His voice roughened on the words, but she thought some of the grief had left his tone, and she took comfort from that. He turned, so that he faced her with only their clasped hands between them. ''What about Peter? Are you still making excuses for him?''

She'd intruded into his life, so it was only fair to answer him as honestly as she could. "I don't know. Maybe I have been."

"He took on responsibility knowingly. He had a duty to carry it through."

"Oddly enough, I don't want to be considered a duty." She tried to say it lightly, but it wasn't easy with his gaze probing into her inner heart.

He lifted his hand slowly and brushed his fingertips along her cheek. The look in his eyes made her breath catch, and she seemed to feel that touch through every single cell of her body.

"Loving you wouldn't be a duty," he said softly. He touched her chin, tilting her face up toward his, and she knew he was going to kiss her.

She shouldn't let this happen. The moment stretched out, frozen in time—the gentleness of Matt's touch, the way his eyes darkened as he looked at her, the treacherous weakness that swept through her.

She should step away. The slightest movement would bring this to an end. She knew Matt well enough to know he'd stop the instant she indicated his embrace wasn't welcome.

She lifted her face, swaying toward him, and his lips met hers.

His kiss was warm and filled with longing, need, desire. His arms went around her strongly, holding her close.

She should pull away. She didn't want to. She wanted to stay within the circle of Matt's embrace and imagine what it would be like to be loved by him, even though her heart knew that could never come true.

Chapter Fourteen

The memory of that kiss warmed Sarah all night and throughout the next morning. She glanced across the office at Matt's desk. His chair was empty, but she could visualize him so clearly, brow furrowed and dark eyes intent, searching for the elusive fact or the right word to make a story come alive.

Giving in to the urge, she crossed to his desk. She did need the events calendar he'd borrowed the day before, didn't she? She wasn't just being silly.

She let her hand rest on the back of his chair. The wood felt warm to the touch, as if he'd just gotten up.

Now, that was silly. Matt hadn't come in to the office at all. He'd just called to say he had something to do and would see her at the house in the afternoon.

Today was the day Andi had been anticipating all

week—the day Matt had promised to let her ride one of the horses. If she'd slept at all last night, it had probably been to dream of galloping through the surf.

Not that Matt would let the children do any galloping, of course. He'd assured Sarah that this was perfectly safe, and she'd be there to make sure they were okay. Her fingers tightened on the chair.

To be honest, she was acting like a teenager in love, mooning over memories of the night before, rehearsing what she'd say when she saw him again. She ought to have more sense at her age.

But somehow, despite her best common sense, she couldn't help but cling to a faint flicker of hope. Maybe this could work out. Maybe…

Maybe she'd better get back to work. She opened the desk drawer and took out the events calendar, revealing something blue and shiny. Her heart lurched. Matt's passport, left handy in his desk drawer in case he wanted it. How foolish was she being, dreaming of family and forever with a man who'd leave again at a moment's notice?

The sound of the door opening came hard on that thought, and she couldn't help the irrational flutter of excitement that stirred her blood. But it wasn't Matt. It was Jason Sanders.

"Good morning, Jason." She smiled at him, shifting gears in an instant. Jason hadn't been in the newspaper office since he'd made the decision to withdraw his advertising. His presence had to be a good sign. Maybe he'd reconsidered.

"Sarah, good to see you." He made it sound as if she'd been avoiding him. He sent a glance toward Matt's desk. "Matt not working here anymore?"

"He's out today." She moved to the counter opposite Jason. "I can have him give you a call later, if you like."

He reached across to pat her hand. "That's all right. I'd much rather talk to a pretty woman."

She resisted the impulse to yank her hand away. The reinstatement of Jason's advertising would go a long way toward easing the paper's financial woes, and she'd do a better job of dealing with him than Matt would.

Of course, when Matt finished his investigation of Jason's real-estate dealings, they might be right back where they'd started. Well, one problem at a time. She fixed a smile on her face.

"How can I help you?"

"You know, Sarah, I've been giving a lot of thought to my decision to take my ads out of the *Gazette*. A lot of thought."

"I'm glad to hear that." She slid her hand from beneath his and reached for a pen. "Nothing would make me happier than to see your advertising back in the paper. After all, we're Caldwell Cove's only newspaper, and your business is certainly important to the local economy."

"Well, now, it would make me happy, too."

She sensed a reservation in his tone, and it lit up warning lights. Sanders sounded like a man about to offer a deal.

"Shall we reinstate your usual ad, then?"

He held up a manicured hand. "Not quite so easy as that, I'm afraid. Before I start paying the *Gazette* for advertising again, I'd want certain reassurances."

Her heart sank. Maybe it was a good thing Matt hadn't come into the office this morning. She could imagine his reaction to that. "Reassurances?"

Sanders leaned toward her, his eyebrows lifting. "Did you two really think I wouldn't get to hear about all the poking around Matt's been doing? Nosing into my business, checking on the property transfers at the county courthouse?"

Apparently someone at the courthouse had been reporting to Sanders. "Matt is a journalist. Naturally he—"

He slammed his hand down hard enough to make her jump. "That doesn't give him the right to interfere with my business. You make him stop, and you'll see my ads back in the *Gazette*." He smiled thinly. "Might even do a full-page once in a while."

There was only one answer to that suggestion. A man with Matt's integrity wouldn't change course for all the full-page ads in the world, and she wouldn't want him to.

"I'm afraid that's impossible. Matt makes the decisions about what stories he'll pursue. Maybe if you explained what you're doing—''

''I'm not about to explain anything to Matt Caldwell.'' His eyes narrowed. ''And you'd better hope I don't have to talk to him, Sarah, or you'll be sorry.''

A shiver ran along her spine at his tone. Something bad was coming; she could feel it. ''I don't know what you mean.''

''I mean I might have to tell Matt about the little arrangement I had with Peter.'' He leaned forward, invading her space. ''You wouldn't want Matt to know your husband took money from me to keep certain matters out of the paper. Now, would you?''

''I—I don't...'' Her mind grappled to come to terms with his words. She wanted to deny it, wanted to say that Peter couldn't possibly have done anything of the kind. The trouble was that, deep in her heart, she feared he could have.

Sanders took a step back, apparently satisfied with the effect of his words. ''Think about it, Sarah. If you don't want Matt and everybody else in this town to know the kind of a man Peter Reed was, you convince Matt to back off.''

He turned and left the office with an assured stride. The door slammed behind him.

The kind of man Peter Reed was. His words echoed in her mind. Sanders wasn't kidding. If she didn't stop Matt's investigation, Sanders would tell him. He'd tell everyone.

But she knew more than Jason Sanders ever could about Matt Caldwell. She knew the kind of man Matt was—a man of integrity, a man who'd never accept the deal Sanders offered and would never understand someone who did. But if he didn't—

She put her hand over her mouth and choked back a sob. If he didn't, the children would know what their father had done. The whole town would know, and things could never be the same. The fragile roots she'd begun to put down for her children would be irrevocably damaged.

She had to tell Matt the truth before Sanders did. But how could she? How could she bear the look on Matt's face when he learned this?

Matt ran the brush down Eagle's silky neck, then patted the horse's strong shoulder. He'd already decided that the boys would have their ride on Jenny's placid pony, but Andi was something different. He had to smile again thinking about the expression on her face when he'd said he'd let her take a ride on Eagle. She'd looked as if an indescribably beautiful gift was within her grasp.

Sarah had looked much the same the night before, when he'd held her in his arms on the Riverwalk. When he'd kissed her and wanted to keep her there forever.

No. Some rational part of his mind still resisted. How could he even let such a thought in? Even if he were sure he loved her, even if she loved him, too much still stood between them.

His life wasn't here, in this quiet backwater. He belonged back in his busy, dangerous world, where there was no room for a man with a family. And there was no point in kidding himself that some kind of long-distance relationship between them would work. Sarah and her kids needed a real husband and father, someone who'd be part of their lives every single day.

That couldn't be him. A wave of something like panic went through him at the thought, and he leaned his forehead against Eagle's warm neck. He couldn't take responsibility for their safety and happiness. His stomach turned as once again he saw the walls of the mission station crumble, heard the children's terrified cries, inhaled the acrid smoke from the bomb.

· The only safe life is a detached life. He repeated the words he'd drummed into his heart.

Once he'd been convinced he could live by them. Now, since he'd met Sarah, he wasn't sure that was possible. He straightened, looked out the open stable door and saw her coming.

"Sarah." Careful, he cautioned himself. Think this through. Don't jump into something that will hurt everyone. The problem was, he didn't want to be careful. He wanted to take her in his arms.

"Hello, Matt." She lingered in the doorway, the sunlight slanting behind her and outlining her figure with gold. Did he just imagine the constraint in her voice?

"The kids are out at the paddock with Wanda and Jenny's pony." He lifted saddle and pad together to Eagle's back. "We'll be ready to go as soon as I finish saddling Eagle."

She came closer. "He still looks awfully big to me. Are you sure it's a good idea to put Andi on his back?"

"He's as gentle as can be." He reached for her hand and felt her swift, instinctive movement away. "I just wanted to show you how to pat him."

His stomach churned. Was that her reaction to what had happened between them the night before? Maybe he didn't need to worry about what he was going to do. Maybe Sarah had already decided this was no good.

"Sorry." She seemed to struggle to produce a smile as she held out her hand.

He took it in his, then smoothed her palm down along the strong, smooth curve of Eagle's neck. His own hand cupped hers, and her sleeve brushed his arm. Awareness seemed to hum between them.

"He's beautiful," she said softly.

He's not the only thing that's beautiful here. He wanted to say the words, but they stuck in his throat. He couldn't say anything.

The moment stretched out. The only sound in the stable was the gentle shuffle of hooves against straw.

Dust motes rose lazily in the shaft of sunlight from the door. Sarah was close enough that her hair brushed his chin, close enough that he could feel her breath. He fought back the impulse to press a kiss to the pulse that throbbed in her neck.

"About yesterday," he said abruptly, needing to put some space between them.

. Her gaze jerked up to meet his, something startled and wary in it. "What about yesterday?"

"I wanted to thank you for going with me to Savannah. I'm not sure I'd have done it without you."

Sudden warmth banished the reserve in her manner. "Of course you would have. But I'm glad I could help." She hesitated, then seemed to decide it was safe to ask what she must be wondering. "Did you tell your father what we found out about Emily?"

"Yes." He turned back to the horse, pulling the girth snug. How much should he reveal to her? Maybe there was no point in trying to hide anything. Sarah had already seen deeper into his heart than anyone else ever had.

"I told him everything." The memory of those moments on the Riverwalk leaped into his mind. "About Emily, I mean."

She nodded, patting Eagle's neck while he slipped the bridle into place. "It was such a sad story. I'm surprised he never made an effort to find out what had become of her."

"Too proud, I'd guess. Caldwells tend to be like

that. But when I told him—'' He hesitated, reliving the look he'd surprised in his father's eyes. "It was years ago. Puppy love, he'd called it. But when I told him what had become of his golden girl, I saw tears in his eyes.''

"She was his first love," Sarah said softly. "You can't forget your first love."

"It wasn't just that." He wanted her to understand. "I've never seen that side of my father. I guess I didn't think it existed. I didn't think he could be moved by anything except business. Seeing him that way—'' He swallowed hard, knowing he needed to tell her the rest of it. "You remember telling me once that you had to go on loving people, even when they disappointed you?''

She nodded, and he saw something that might almost have been hope in her eyes. "I remember."

"I guess I finally understand what that means." He shrugged, embarrassed at the way emotion had thickened his voice. "I think my father and I have started to come to terms with each other. Thanks to you.''

"I didn't have much to do with it. You were ready. Maybe that's really why you came home."

He wanted to tell her that she'd changed him, but he couldn't seem to find the words and wasn't sure he should say them if he did. "I don't suppose things will ever be the way they were before, when I was Jeffrey's age and thought my father was a hero. But it's better now. I feel…'' He searched for the word. "Comfortable. I feel comfortable here now."

He wasn't sure what he wanted her to say to that, but she just nodded. "I'm glad." She clasped his hand briefly, then moved a step toward the door, into the patch of sunlight.

Something tightened inside him, making it impossible to speak. The words he'd said about his father echoed in his mind. Maybe it was true he'd never see his father as a hero again. But he couldn't help longing, no matter how foolish it was, that Sarah saw him that way.

She had to tell him. She couldn't. Sarah leaned against the paddock fence, watching Matt with her children. What was she going to do?

For a moment, when Matt had talked about loving his father in spite of his faults, she'd felt a spurt of hope. Maybe he was learning that sometimes love could break through his rigid expectations of people.

Things will never be the way they were before, he'd said, and the words had shattered that fledgling hope. When he knew the truth about what Peter had done—well, he might be able to accept the fact that she hadn't known about it. But he wouldn't be able to forget. And if she asked him to compromise his beliefs, let Sanders off the hook to protect her family…

He wouldn't agree. He couldn't. And even if he did, things would never be the same between them.

Help me, Lord. Her fingers tightened on the rough wooden plank until it bit into her skin. *I don't know what to do. How can I be honest with Matt and still protect my children from knowing what Peter did? How can I?*

She took a breath, trying to clear her mind, trying to listen for God's guidance, but nothing came. Maybe that silence in itself was her answer. She couldn't.

"Mommy, look at me!" Ethan waved wildly as Matt led him past on the black-and-white pony.

Matt gently put Ethan's hand back on the reins. "You can't let go, or Dolly won't know what you want her to do. You're the rider, so you're the responsible one, okay?"

Ethan clutched the reins, nodding solemnly. "Okay. I'll remember."

The scene caught her heart in a painful grip. Ethan was so like Peter in his manner. He needed the example a strong, honest man could provide to show him what it meant to be a man.

There was Jeffrey, arms draped over the lowest rail of the fence, waiting so patiently for it to be his turn. Jeffrey had blossomed under Matt's attention. He'd begun speaking for himself instead of letting Ethan talk for him. Jeffrey needed someone like Matt, too.

Why wasn't this meant to be, Lord? It seems so right.

She watched, not moving or speaking, while Matt

took Jeffrey for his ride. Then, finally, it was Andi's turn. When Matt helped her little girl onto the big horse, tension gripped Sarah. It was so far to the ground. Surely that horse was too much for Andi.

But Matt was slow, confident, sure as he showed Andi how to hold the reins, how to cluck to the animal. Everything about him radiated competence. Andi was safe with him.

And as for Andi—when Jenny swung easily into the pony's saddle and the girls moved off at a walk side by side, Andi's face was suffused with so much joy that Sarah wanted to weep.

Matt's eyes never left the girls as he walked slowly across to lean on the fence next to her. "Looks like she was born to ride," he said.

She swallowed the lump in her throat. "You've just made all her dreams come true."

"Probably not all of them," he said. He propped his elbows behind him on the fence, the movement stretching his shirt across his chest. His forearm brushed hers, sending a wave of warmth up her arm.

Jeffrey trotted up next to her. "Can I have another turn, Matt? Please?"

"We might be able to do that." Matt reached through the fence to pick the boy up, swinging him into his arms and then setting him on the top rail of the fence. Jeffrey perched there, breathless and grinning at him.

Her throat tightened again. Jeffrey opened like a

flower to the sun when Matt was around. Why hadn't she realized how much he needed a man's attention?

A father's attention. The words slipped into her mind and she had trouble ejecting them. Matt gave her glimpses of a different relationship—one where she didn't have to shoulder all the burdens. One where love and responsibility could be equally shared. But even if it weren't for the knowledge of Peter's misdeeds, weighing heavy on her heart, too many barriers existed to a serious relationship with Matt.

Matt would leave. That was the bottom line. He'd always intended to go back to his important job. And when he found out what an ethical dilemma his partnership with her had landed him in, he'd probably race to leave as soon as he could.

Matt nudged her with his elbow. "I want to talk with you about the real-estate investigation. Why don't I stop by after the kids are in bed?"

Panic surged through her. If they talked about his investigation of Sanders, she'd have to tell him. She should have told him already, but she couldn't. She hadn't figured out how.

"Tonight's not good for me." She hoped her voice didn't sound as strangled as it felt. "Maybe tomorrow morning would be better."

She felt Matt's gaze on her face, questioning, and kept her own focused firmly on the horses. If he asked what was so important she couldn't meet with him tonight, what would she say?

He shrugged finally. "Okay. Tomorrow morning."

She should feel relieved, but she didn't. She'd only bought a few more hours in which to find a way to tell him about Peter. A few hours in which to enjoy the relationship that was doomed to end once she told him the truth.

Chapter Fifteen

A mostly sleepless night spent in prayer had shown Sarah what she had to do, little though she might like it. She had to be honest with Matt. He was her partner, and he had a right to know what Peter had done and what Sanders demanded of them.

Matt would never agree to Sanders's terms. She knew that without even thinking about it.

She glanced around the small apartment that was so precious to her. She could hear the children's voices in the kitchen with the sitter, smell the potpourri she'd put in the Delft bowl on the mantel, see the love she'd poured into making this place a home. Once everyone in Caldwell Cove knew that her husband had traded the newspaper's integrity for money, what were the chances she could still call this home?

Please, Lord, let us find some way of making this work out. Let us find a resolution that—

She stopped, knowing what she wanted to pray. She wanted to ask that somehow she and Matt and the children could become a family.

She couldn't ask that. She couldn't even let herself dream it. Even if there were no problem with Sanders, a relationship between them had been doomed from the start. Matt's life was elsewhere. He hadn't deceived her about that. He'd never be content with this life, and she had to put her children's security first. There was no compromise that would make them both happy.

Enough. She forced herself to move toward the door into the office. Matt was there; she'd heard him arrive. She just had to stop agonizing about it and go in there and tell him.

Stomach churning, she opened the door and stepped through, feeling as if she walked knowingly into a nightmare.

"Good morning." Matt looked up from his computer, a slow smile lighting his face as his gaze rested on her. "I thought maybe you were sleeping in this morning."

"No, I just…I was running a little late." It was the smile that hurt, she decided. The smile blindsided her with how much she'd grown to care for him.

Not just care. She'd better be honest with herself about that. She loved him.

She hadn't seen it coming. She'd thought she was safely armored against loving again. The children were her life now, and she didn't need anything else. But she loved him.

She took a deep breath. That couldn't make a difference in what she had to do. She had to tell him. "Matt, there's something I need to—"

"Take a look at this first." He gestured to the computer screen. "I've found it."

"Found what?" She went to his desk, leaning over his chair so she could read what was on the screen. Her hand brushed against his shoulder, and she snatched it back as if she'd been burned.

"Found the smoking gun." Triumph laced Matt's voice. "I know what Sanders has been doing down at the end of the island. He's been buying up parcels of land under different names, so no one would get wise. And he's negotiating to sell the whole thing to a commercial cannery."

"But…" Her mind whirled with the implications of that. "An outfit like that tried to come in a few years ago, and people made such a fuss that the town council blocked it. Nobody wanted a commercial outfit here, ruining the atmosphere and taking all the fish—that was the only thing the summer people and the islanders ever agreed on in their lives. How could Sanders hope to get it through now?"

"At a guess, he's got someone from the town council in his pocket. If he keeps it quiet until the permits have been granted, there won't be much anyone can do."

She nodded slowly, thinking about her guess that Sanders had an informant at the county courthouse. That was certainly the way he operated. And if it were true—

"Do you have facts?" she asked abruptly. "Solid, verifiable evidence?"

Matt lifted an eyebrow. "Worried about being sued? Don't be. There's enough here to stop Sanders in his tracks without any fear of that."

The implacable determination in his face chilled her. His was the face of a crusader. He wouldn't stop until he'd put every last fact on the front page.

"Matt, I want to tell you something." She gripped the chair back, trying to find the words. "There's something you need to know."

The tone of her voice must have penetrated his focus. He shifted away from the computer to face her, and his hand covered hers. "What is it? What's wrong?"

She could hardly bear the concern in his face. She had to tell him—now.

The office door swung open. Jason Sanders stepped in, looking from one to the other of them. Then he smiled. "I hope I'm not interrupting anything."

The change in Matt vibrated through the air between them. In an instant he went from tender and caring to ready to battle.

"Not at all." Matt's calm, businesslike tone didn't hide the intensity beneath from her. "What can we do for you?"

Nothing, she wanted to cry. Just leave, that's all, and let me deal with this in my own way.

Panic cut through her like a knife. Sanders had come for their capitulation. She'd run out of time to tell Matt. Now he'd learn the truth in the worst possible way.

Jason sauntered to the counter as if he owned the place. "Just thought you might have something to tell me today."

"Tell you?" Matt's level brows lifted. "About what?" He leaned back in his chair, assuming a casual air he couldn't really be feeling, not when his evidence against Sanders spread across the computer screen in front of him.

Sanders glanced from Matt to her and back again. "I see your partner didn't confide in you."

Her panic edged up a notch. "I haven't had time to talk with Matt about it yet. If you'd like to come back later—"

Matt swiveled his chair to look at her. "What's going on, Sarah? Talk to me about what?"

"Just a little deal I offered Sarah." Sanders's tone spoke of his confidence that he would get what he wanted.

"You always have a deal to offer, Jason. Trouble is, they usually only benefit you. You haven't changed in twenty years.'' The contempt in Matt's voice seemed to dent Sanders's assurance, and Sarah saw the flare of anger in his eyes.

''Matt, I don't think—'' She put her hand warningly on his shoulder.

''Still the white knight riding to the rescue, aren't you, Caldwell? You'll find it simple to rescue Sarah, actually. All you have to do is drop this little investigation of yours.''

Matt's tension tightened his shoulders. ''In exchange for what?''

The truth rolled toward Sarah like a boulder, flattening everything in its path.

''In exchange for my silence. Somehow I don't think Sarah wants the world to know that her late husband took payoffs to keep my business affairs out of the paper.'' Sanders smiled. ''Actually, I don't suppose you want it to come out either. It would reflect rather badly on the *Gazette*. Might even tarnish that fine reputation of yours, since you're a part owner.''

She wanted to close her eyes and shut out the look Matt gave her. But she couldn't.

''Sarah, is this true?''

She couldn't speak. She could only nod.

Matt looked at her steadily for a long moment. Then he turned away.

She wanted to cry out, to tell him she was sorry, to say she hadn't known. But what good would it do, even if she could find the words? Matt wouldn't give in to Sanders. She'd known that all along. Truth came first with Matt. He'd never deny that.

"Making that public will hurt you as much as it will us." Matt's voice was icy.

Sanders shrugged. "If you print what you know, the sweetest deal I ever had is gone. Seems like a wash to me. I may as well take you down with me."

Matt stood, planting his fists on the desk, so rigid he might have been a statue instead of a man. He'd reject Sanders's deal. And then he'd reject her. She'd lost whatever small chance their relationship had because she hadn't told him herself.

"All right. You have a deal." Matt's words dropped into the silence, sending ripples through the room.

His agreement echoed in her mind. She couldn't believe it. Why would Matt give in?

"I'm glad we understand each other." Sanders seemed to be enjoying this. "You wouldn't want people to lose respect for the hotshot television reporter, now would you?"

That wasn't why Matt had agreed. She knew that as clearly as if she could see right into his mind. Matt had given in, had compromised his most cherished beliefs, in order to protect her and her children.

She couldn't let him do it. Through the chaos in her thoughts, that one thing stood clear, shining like a beacon. She'd asked God to show her what was right, and God had done that in the clearest possible way. She couldn't let Matt be false to himself to help her. It would be the worst betrayal in the world.

"No." Her sharp tone had both men turning to face her. "We won't do it."

"Sarah—" Matt's tone was warning.

"What do you mean, you won't do it?" Sanders clearly didn't believe her.

"Just what I said." She walked to the counter, hanging on to her composure with both hands. "We don't agree to your terms. We won't keep silent."

Sanders looked as if she'd snatched away a promised treat. "I mean what I say. I'll make my dealings with your husband public. I won't have anything to lose."

But I do. Despair threatened to overwhelm her. The respect of the community, her children's view of their father, maybe even the home she'd tried to build here. And she'd already lost Matt.

Do the right thing. She clung to the thought. She looked steadily at Sanders. "The story will be on the front page of tomorrow's paper. Including your deal with Peter."

Fury darkened his face. For a moment she thought he'd threaten again. Then he spun and stalked out.

The slamming door seemed to break the strength that held her upright. She sagged against the counter. It was over.

No, it wasn't over, not yet. Pain ripped through her. Her children, her home...and Matt. The pain of letting him down cut the deepest. She turned slowly to face him.

"Matt, I want to explain—" The look in his eyes seemed to choke off her voice.

"Why didn't you tell me?" He ground the words out.

"I didn't know until yesterday. You have to believe that."

He looked at her as if she were a stranger, and his square jaw was set in the way that denied compromise. "You knew about this yesterday, and you didn't trust me enough to tell me."

"I tried. I wanted to. I just couldn't. Matt, please try to understand—"

He shook his head. "I have to go." He strode quickly to the door. "Do what you want about tomorrow's issue, Sarah. It's up to you." He was out the door before she could speak.

He had to go. Her heart shattered into pieces. He'd left the island before when his father hadn't lived up to his ideals. She'd just given him the perfect reason to leave again.

"But, Mommy, why does it have to be in the paper? It would hurt Daddy's feelings." Andi looked small against her pillows. Sarah had found her still awake when she'd come wearily back into the apartment from the office after working late into the evening.

She stroked fine blond hair away from Andi's face. "Honey, I think Daddy would want us to tell the whole story now, even if it hurts." The two boys had accepted the short version she'd told them, not realizing that this story could have an effect on their lives. But Andi couldn't be content with that.

"People will talk about it. They might say mean things about Daddy." Andi's mouth trembled. "I don't want that to happen."

"I know," she said. "Neither do I."

The headache that clamped around her temples throbbed, and she massaged her neck wearily. She'd worked for hours to reset the front page. For a time, she'd half thought Matt might come back to do his story.

Finally she'd given up and done it for him, using his notes. Matt wouldn't be back—she had to face that. It brought a fresh wave of pain.

"Listen, Andi." She ought to be able to think of a way of explaining this that would satisfy her daughter. "If we don't put the story in the paper, then someone else will get away with doing something that's really wrong. We can't let that happen. That would be like helping that person do wrong."

Andi's forehead wrinkled. "You mean, it's like what Matt said when I tried to cover up for Ethan and Jeffrey? He said it would hurt them more if I took the blame than if they owned up to it."

Regret clutched her heart. "Yes, I guess it's like that. Matt was right." About so many things.

"When's Matt coming back?" Andi wiggled restlessly against the pillow. "I want to see him."

"I don't know when he's coming back, honey." Maybe never. She should try to prepare the children for that possibility, however much it might lacerate her already-wounded heart.

"You know, Matt has another job, being on television." She was improvising, trying to come up with something that wouldn't hurt too much. "He might have to go away to do that job, but then you could see him on television. Wouldn't that be fun?"

Andi shook her head stubbornly. "Not as much fun as having him here every day."

"No." A dozen pictures flickered through her mind—working at the desk next to Matt; listening to his grandmother's stories with him; trudging through Savannah on the trail of the truth; standing close in the circle of his arms while a boat whistle blew a lonely accompaniment. "It won't be as much fun. But Matt might have to go away."

Andi was still shaking her head. "No, Mommy, he won't go away. I know he won't. Know why?"

Sarah touched her cheek gently. "Tell me why, sweetheart."

"'Cause he said he'd take me and Jenny riding again, that's why. He promised us. And Matt wouldn't ever break a promise.'' She leaned back against the pillow, satisfied.

Pain was a vise around her heart. She'd not only let herself in for the hurt of losing Matt. She'd let the children in for it, too.

She stared out the window, watching the last rays of sunlight paint the sky. Where are you, Matt? What are you feeling?

She might not know where he was, but Someone did. *Father, forgive me. My silence hurt so many people. Please be with Matt now. Touch his heart and heal it. Amen.*

Chapter Sixteen

The sun was setting when Matt pushed open the door to the church. He let it swing slowly closed behind him, not sure why he was here. He slid into a back pew, avoiding a sidelong look at the stained-glass window of Jesus and the children.

After he'd left the office, he'd saddled Eagle and ridden the beach until he and the horse were both exhausted. Eagle had been content once he was back in his quiet stall with his feed bag. Matt found he wasn't so easily satisfied.

Finally he'd started throwing things into a suitcase. Leave, get on the road again, find a place where the action would blank everything else out of his mind. That was all he could think. He had to go back to being his old, detached self.

Then he'd driven past the chapel and stopped the

car, almost without intent. Here he was, trying to run away again. Maybe that had been excusable when he'd been eighteen and trying to escape his father's shadow. It wasn't excusable now.

He leaned forward, propping his wrists on the pew in front of him and leaning his head against his forearms. The silence in the chapel leached the tension from him, and for the first time in hours he was able to look past emotion and assess what had happened.

Sarah should have told you, something in his mind whispered righteously. *She owed you the truth.*

Truth. He'd never been able to take the elastic view of that some people did. But Sarah— She had to have been shaken and appalled when she'd found out what her late husband had done. Knowing Sarah, she'd probably felt guilty, too, that she hadn't somehow been able to prevent it.

He knew her now, knew her bone-deep, knew her warmth and her caring. When he'd been hurting over his father's actions, she'd reached out with unquestioning support.

Today she'd needed support, and he'd walked away. The realization shamed him.

You have to go on loving people, even when they disappoint you. She'd said that. It was the way she lived her life. He admired that, but he wasn't sure he could do it.

He could leave. He could get in the car, drive to Savannah and hop on a plane to anywhere in the world. If his bosses weren't ready to let him come back, he could look for a job elsewhere—any job that would let him observe, report and, above all, not get involved.

He rubbed his face with his hands. He'd tried that. He'd come back here determined to do it. But Sarah and her kids hadn't let him. Their faces crowded his mind—Andi, determined and responsible; Ethan, needing a man to look up to; Jeffrey, wanting encouragement to be himself; little Amy, the unknown quantity with the engaging smile.

And Sarah. How could he walk away from Sarah's boundless love? But how could he stay and make himself responsible for their happiness?

The familiar image of the bombed-out mission pressed on him like a weight, until it felt as if his heart would burst. *Why, God? Why did You let that happen? Why?*

He knew what some of his colleagues would say. That there was no God, that people were at the mercy of random fate. In a way, that might be a comfortable belief, because they didn't have to question. He didn't have that luxury.

Why? He jerked upright, forcing himself to look at the window he'd avoided. *How could You let Your children be hurt?*

The children clustered around Jesus, looking up at him. The final rays of the setting sun struck the window, making the pictured face glow with a love so pure and intense that it seemed to pierce his heart, cutting clear through, letting the pain spurt out.

Sarah's words came back to him, echoing in the stillness as if she were there, speaking them. *God isn't to blame for the bad things. People are. But God can bring good out of them, if we let Him.*

His throat was tight with pain. Bad things, like the injured children, like his friend's death, like the guilt that had driven him home. He looked again at Jesus and the children, and the tears he'd tried so hard not to shed spilled over in a healing stream.

Sarah stared at the telephone on her desk the next morning. The paper had been out for two hours. Wasn't it time for reactions to start coming in? She'd expected the phone to be ringing off the hook with people canceling their subscriptions.

Not that she wanted that to happen. But anything would be better than this silence. Silence gave her too much time to think about Matt.

If she thought about him she couldn't avoid the pain. She pressed her fist to her chest. Why did this hurt so much? She'd known all along that nothing could come of their relationship. She should have been prepared. At the moment, that thought gave her no comfort.

Be with me, Lord. No matter what comes, let me feel Your presence.

The telephone rang. She took a deep breath, composed herself and picked it up. "*Caldwell Cove Gazette*. How may I help you?"

She'd prepared herself for canceled subscriptions. She hadn't been prepared for renewals. But in the next half hour, over a dozen people called to extend their subscriptions.

While she was still trying to figure that out, the door opened. Her heart clenched at the sight of the tall figure, but it wasn't Matt. Of course it wasn't Matt. Instead, his brother, Adam, came in with new copy for an ad for the boatyard.

He'd barely gone out when Tracy Milburn came in with an ad for the bakery, followed by Josh Tremain wanting to buy an ad for his tackle shop. By noon, she'd sold more ad space in one morning than she'd sold in the entire last month.

Somehow she wasn't surprised when Matt's grandmother trotted into the office, holding an ad for the upcoming church rummage sale. Her throat tight, Sarah held up the sheaf of orders.

"Are you responsible for this, Mrs. Caldwell?"

Naomi Caldwell pulled herself to her five-foot height. "Me? Why would you think that?"

Sarah blinked back an errant tear that had no place in a business office. "Seems as if everyone in Caldwell Cove wants to place an ad or renew a subscription today. I get the feeling someone might have put them up to it."

Mrs. Caldwell shrugged, a twinkle in her sharp blue

eyes. "Folks here appreciate courage. I reckon they wanted to show you that. After all, you're one of us."

The tears did spill over, then. "My husband—"

"Nobody blames you for what your husband did," Matt's gran said tartly.

Sarah shook her head. "I know there must be some who think I had to have known about it."

"More fool they, then." Naomi Caldwell patted her hand firmly. "Folks who know you know different. The others don't matter. You just remember that and hold your head up high."

"I'll try." Sarah managed a watery smile.

"And don't you shed tears over that fool grandson of mine. That boy's starting to find himself. He's just still got a way to go." A shadow bisected the sunlight streaming through the door, and she glanced toward it. Her face softened. "Or maybe he's finally found his way home."

She bustled out, giving Matt a pat on his shoulder as she passed him in the doorway. She closed the door, and Matt stood there, motionless, for a long moment.

Sarah couldn't speak. She wanted to, but she couldn't. She could only look at him, knowing her love must show plainly in her face.

He moved toward her at last, holding up a copy of the paper. "I saw the front page. Looks good. You must have worked until midnight."

"Not quite that late." If he wanted to keep this

exchange on business, she'd have to try, no matter how much it hurt.

He came around the counter, dropping the paper on it. "You used my byline."

"It was your story. I just wrote it up."

"I understand the town council has already called an emergency meeting. Somehow I think Jason Sanders isn't going to get his way this time."

It was no good—she couldn't try to pretend they were just coeditors, discussing a story that had gone well.

"Matt, I'm sorry. I should never have—"

"Don't, Sarah." He put his hand across her lips, his touch gentle. "I understand why it was hard to tell me. What happened wasn't your fault."

"I should have known," she managed to say, her lips moving against his palm. "And I should have told you as soon as I found out. That was my mistake."

He took her hands in both of his then, and his look was so intent that it seemed he saw right into her soul. "We both made mistakes. Maybe—" He smiled slightly. "Maybe we needed to, so that God could teach us something."

Her heart seemed to swell. If this painful time had made Matt turn back to God, it would have been well worth it.

"What did you learn?" she asked softly, hardly daring to believe it.

"That truth isn't anything without love," he said readily. "That I can find God's hand moving, even in the midst of pain." His voice roughened. "You taught me that, Sarah. Without you, I'd never have healed."

"You're okay now." She tried to keep her voice steady, tried not to let her broken heart show. "You're ready to go back."

"I could go back. But that doesn't seem as important as it once did." He gestured toward the paper. "Seems as if I can find important stories to tell here." He gripped her hands tightly. "Seems as if I can find someone to force me back into life here. Wouldn't I be a fool to let that end?"

All of his honest, valiant heart showed in the look he gave her. The intimacy and power of it robbed her of any ability to speak.

"Well, Sarah?" His voice had grown husky. "Will you let me be a father to your children? Will you let me be your husband?"

She still couldn't speak. Could she? Did she really have it in herself to be the person who loved him and was loved in return?

A sense of freedom swept over her. The past was gone. This was a new world for both of them. She stepped into his arms and knew that, like him, she'd found home.

"Matt!" The door to the apartment swung open, and Andi ran in. "See, Mommy, I told you he would come back.'' She raced to him, the two boys scurrying after her.

Matt knelt, gathering them into a hug. Amy toddled proudly across the floor, testing her new skill, and he swept her up into his arms.

''Well, Sarah?'' He looked at her, face alight with love and confidence. ''You still haven't answered me.''

''Yes.'' Her heart seemed to overflow with gratitude. ''The answer is yes, for all of us.'' She blinked back tears of joy. She'd made mistakes, but God had been faithful. He'd given her a man of integrity, a man she and her children could love and trust for all their days.

Epilogue

"Can't I take the blindfold off yet?" Sarah gripped Matt's hand as he guided her up the steps.

He grinned, wondering where she thought they were. He hoped he'd covered his tracks well, but it was tough to fool Sarah.

"Not yet, Mrs. Caldwell." He tried to keep the excitement out of his voice and failed. "I have a surprise for you."

"I think two weeks in Hawaii for our honeymoon was enough of a surprise."

"Didn't you enjoy it?" He pressed his cheek against hers.

"I loved it." She reached up to caress the planes of his face, and he dropped a kiss on her fingertips. "But now I'm ready to be home."

"Right." They reached the porch, and he scooped

Sarah off her feet and into his arms. "Your wish is granted." He took several steps forward, across the threshold, and set her on her feet.

"Matt, what's going on?"

He fumbled with the blindfold, and it fell away. "You're home."

Miz Becky, who'd been holding the children back, let them go, and they rushed, giggling, into her arms. She knelt, clutching them close. He suspected she didn't see anything else.

"See, Mommy, see?" Andi broke free first, hopping on one foot and then the other. "See? It's our new house. Isn't it beautiful?" She darted to the tall Gullah woman who stood smiling near the doorway. "Miz Becky helped us fix it all up, and I have my own room with horses on the wallpaper."

"Our house?"

Sarah turned slowly, and Matt realized he was holding his breath. He saw the moment she recognized where they were—in one of the new houses on the lane behind Twin Oaks. But it no longer stood empty. Sarah's furniture, supplemented with pieces from the big house, filled the living room, and her pictures were on the walls.

She was quiet for so long that uncertainty assailed him.

"If you don't like it—" he began.

"Like it?" she echoed. She looked at him, a smile trembling on her lips, tears filling her eyes, and he

knew it was all right. "I don't just like it. I love it."
Her arms went around his waist, and she leaned into
him. "I love it," she repeated softly. "I love you."

Andi danced back to them. "The whole family
helped, Mommy. All the aunts and uncles and cousins. And Gran. And Grandfather Jeff." Andi proudly
enumerated all the relatives she'd inherited on her
mother's marriage.

Their family. His family. He looked at his Sarah,
surrounded by their children. "Are you sure you like
it?"

"How could I not like it?" She leaned into his
embrace. "It's our home."

"*Home.*" He repeated the word.

He'd come back to Caldwell Island hoping to regain his detachment, thinking that was what he
wanted. But instead God had given him what he
needed—love and a home.

*…in all things, God works for the good of those
who love Him…* His heart overflowed with thanks-
giving. Gran's promise for him had finally come true.

*　*　*　*　*

*Will Adam Caldwell
get a second chance at love?
Find out in
A TIME TO FORGIVE,
coming only to
Love Inspired in December 2002.
And now for a sneak preview,
please turn the page.*

Chapter One

Adam Caldwell stared, appalled, at the woman who'd just swung a sledgehammer at his carefully ordered life. "What did you say?"

The slight tightening of her lips indicated impatience. "Your mother-in-law hired me to create a memorial window for your late wife." Her gesture took in the quiet interior of the Caldwell Island church, with its ancient stained-glass windows glowing in the slanting October sunlight, its rows of pews empty on a weekday afternoon. "Here."

He'd always prided himself on keeping his head in difficult situations. He certainly needed that poise now, when pain had such a grip on his throat that it was hard to speak. He put a hand on the warm, smooth wood of a pew back and turned to Pastor

Wells, whose call had brought him rushing from the boatyard in the middle of a workday.

"Do you know anything about this?"

The pastor beamed, brushing a lock of untidy graying hair back from his forehead. "Only what Ms. Marlowe has been telling me. Isn't it wonderful, Adam? Mrs. Telforth has offered to fund not only the new window, but the repairs on all the existing windows. God has answered our prayers."

If God had answered Henry Wells's prayers in this respect, He'd certainly been ignoring Adam's. Adam glanced back at the woman who stood beneath the largest of the church's windows, its jewel colors highlighting her pale face. She was watching him with a challenge in her dark eyes, as if she knew exactly how he felt about the idea of a memorial to Lila.

She couldn't. Nobody could know that.

He summed up his impressions of the woman—a tangle of dark brown curls falling to her shoulders, brown eyes under straight, determined brows, a square, stubborn chin. Her tan slacks, white shirt and navy blazer seemed designed to let her blend into any setting, but she still looked out of place on this South Carolina sea island. Slight, she nevertheless had the look of a person who'd walk over anything in her path. Right now, that anything was him.

"Well, now, Ms.—" He stopped, making it a question.

"Marlowe," she said. "Tory Marlowe."

"Yes." He glanced at the card she'd handed him. Marlowe Stained Glass Studio, Philadelphia. Not far from his mother-in-law's place in New Jersey. Maybe that was the connection between them. "Ms. Marlowe. Caldwell Island's a long way from home for you." His South Carolina drawl was a deliberate contrast to the briskness she'd shown. A slow, courteous stone wall—that was what was called for here. "Seems kind of funny, you showing up out of the blue like this."

She lifted those level brows, as if acknowledging an adversary, and he thought her long fingers tightened on the leather bag she carried. "Mrs. Telforth gave me a commission. I came."

"Also seems kind of funny that my mother-in-law didn't get in touch with me first."

Actually, it didn't, but he wasn't about to tell this stranger that. Mona Telforth blew in and out of his life, and his daughter's life, like a shower of palm leaves ripped by a storm—here unexpectedly, gone almost as quickly.

"I wouldn't know anything about that, but she spelled out her wishes quite clearly." The overhead fan moved the sultry air and ruffled the woman's hair. "She asked me to create a window that will be a tribute to her daughter's life and memory."

Pain clenched again, harder this time. Mona Telforth didn't know everything about her daughter's life. She never would. He'd protect her memories of

Lila, but he wouldn't walk into this sanctuary every Sunday and look at a window memorializing a lie. Which meant that Tory Marlowe, with her determined air and her lonely eyes, had to go back to where she belonged.

Dear Reader,

Thank you for choosing to read *A Mother's Wish*. I hope you enjoy the love story of Matthew Caldwell, his Sarah and her four rambunctious children.

This story has floated around in the back of my mind for a long time. I wasn't sure what it would be, but I knew it had to involve an embittered man who blamed God for all the wrongs in the world. And I knew he'd find his way back to God through the love of a nurturing woman and her little family. Matt and Sarah began to come to life for me, and here is their story.

Please let me know how you like this story. I'd love to send you a signed bookplate and let you know about future releases. Write to me at Steeple Hill Books, 300 East 42nd Street, New York, NY 10017, or visit me on the Web at www.martaperry.com.

Blessings,

Marta Perry

Next Month From Steeple Hill''s

Love Inspired®

Midnight Faith
by
Gena Dalton

Taciturn cowboy Clint McMahan liked life the way it
was—peaceful and women free. So when a headstrong
beauty wanted to start a riding school on *his ranch* he
wasn't keen on the idea. But before long she opened a
whole new world to the disillusioned bachelor....

Don't miss
MIDNIGHT FAITH

On sale October 2002

LIMF

Next Month From Steeple Hill's

Love Inspired

Family Ties

by

Bonnie K. Winn

Widow Flynn Mallory never guessed he'd relocate to a
sleepy town like Rosewood, let alone set foot in church
after all these years. Even more miraculous, he and his
pint-size triplets felt right at home there, thanks to his
kindhearted former sister-in-law, Cindy Thompson.
Was the one thing Flynn needed to heal his battered
heart closer than he'd ever imagined?

Don't miss
FAMILY TIES

On sale September 2002

Love Inspired

Next Month From Steeple Hill®'s

Love Inspired®

Mountain Laurel
by
Kate Welsh

No romantic fool, CJ Larson didn't feel instant
attraction to anyone—least of all a decidedly *unspiritual*
heartbreaker with a lady-killer grin. But the spunky
horse trainer couldn't deny the electricity zinging between
her and handsome veterinarian Cole Taggert any more
than she could deny her own steadfast faith....

**Don't miss
MOUNTAIN LAUREL**
On sale October 2002